American Cockroach

Nick Vukmanovich and Sharon Anderson

ISBN-13: 978-0-692-11470-4

INTRODUCTION

I interviewed Nick Vukmanovich and Sharon Anderson about their novel "American Cockroach", a novel based on a combination of truth and fantasy. Their audience will realize that this is mad poetry, a hidden symphonic movement of punk philosophy. We eventually met at the Pig n' Whistle in Los Angeles, CA. Two weeks ago I sat for hours at an outdoor table at Spago in Beverly Hills waiting for the duo to show up for this interview. I tried to get them to meet me at the Chateau Marmont last week, but again they never showed. I was beginning to think I wouldn't be able to unravel the mystery of American Cockroach, and I was also beginning to suspect that these two individuals weren't real, either.

I secured a table in the back near the bar, and from that vantage point I saw a back lit figure emerge through the front door. He was muttering to himself while lighting a cigarette and wore paint spattered jeans and three long sleeved shirts turned inside out. I sensed this was Vukmanovich, and I was right. He refused to take off his sunglasses even though the bar was dark and it was early evening. When I asked why he was wearing his clothes inside out, he said it was to ward off evil spirits. We exchanged a few pleasantries and waited for his counterpart.

Suddenly we were blinded by refracted squares of light dancing over the surfaces of the interior as though a disco ball had entered the bar. Anderson had shown up in a silver glitter body suit complete with platform shoes and a pink feather boa. Large sunglasses reminiscent of early 70's Elton John dwarfed her face. Nick said "This is why we need panes. The mirror ball effect."

After asking Anderson for her ID, Vukmanovich appeared agitated. "Cosmo," he said, "I get it that you need to see my ID, but hers? Shouldn't you already know what Sharon looks like from the San

Francisco newspaper world?" "Good point, Nick. But you already know that photography conveys image and not presence, and besides, photography is a lie and people have a thousand faces." At that point he was ordering drinks and ignoring me. He looked at Anderson and said "Are you on your period?" She replied, unfazed, "No, what are you picking up?" I can't figure out this line of questioning and I blurted out "What the hell?" Sharon explained. "You don't understand. Nick has the olfactory ability to sense menstruation from 20 feet. It's a gift, like the fact that I can hum and whistle at the same time." Nick shot me a look and said "Maybe you're the one bleeding, Cosmo." I had to reluctantly admit I'd just had hemorrhoid surgery. "In that case, avoid the lobster fra diavolo," Nick replied.

CS: You both have been working on this novel, writing together nearly every day for the last six months. Let's get into it, when you started writing this book during Labor Day weekend of 2017, you were strangers. How did that happen?

NV: We are still strangers.

SA: We both knew we were painters and writers and that was enough. Perhaps.

NV: What's the worst thing that could happen?

SA: Strangers equals a clean slate. No baggage.

CS: Let's sort the drink order. Nick this one's yours, not mine. A shot and a beer and be sure to hand Sharon her absinthe. The cosmopolitan is mine, thanks. Anyway, I was interested in the twists and turns of American Cockroach. This novel starts like a noir crime story but quickly goes sideways into parts unknown. The narrative erodes into fragments, first and third person, time jumping, fantasy, poetry...The structure is a little unconventional. I was under the impression that the two main characters Billy Ball and Nancy Masterson were fiction, but you say they actually exist?

NV: Billy and Masterson, that's all true. Everything in the book is true.

CS: Yes, but you have a magic realist influence too, you have to admit. The time travel portions for example. The dream sequences.

SA: That's real, too. Time travel and dreams. Just because you can't get there yourself...

NV: God had two children, Jesus and Candy. It's all in the book.

SA: At the beginning of the writing project, we both read The Third Mind by William Burroughs and Brion Gysin. This became a template of sorts for the whole process.

NV: The combination of two thoughts, two minds, and two sets of efforts gives birth to the Third Mind. That's ultimately who wrote the book, not us.

CS: That makes sense, a writing methodology for painters. The main characters, Billy and Nancy, seem to have a severe crisis of identity over time.

SA: Yes. They both also emerge as unreliable narrators. Billy and Nancy remember events very differently.

CS: That's true, there are different versions of reality and the reader has to decide what to believe. And all the characters, by the way, seem very violent, crass and bigoted. It's relentless. Why add that tension?

NV: It's honest. This book is about America.

SA: People ARE violent, crass and bigoted.

CS: Interspersed in the narrative are third person observations that seem fantastical and take us out of the main story, the first person accounts of Billy and Nancy. This happens more frequently as the story moves toward the ending. Who is this third person voice?

SA: Consciousness is a stream and when you look at it, there's garbage floating around in there. These are the facts of daily life. Surrealism is everywhere, you just have to notice it. Just the other day I was awakened by my phone playing George Harrison's "My Sweet Lord" while simultaneously showing me an advertisement for a Prius. I was still pondering that advertising algorithm as I drove over a canyon in my not-Prius. Next to the road I saw a remote control police car crashed into a rock. Barbie dolls dressed like cops were also strewn about the vicinity. What did it mean? I'll never solve that mystery. If it wasn't such a dangerous, narrow canyon road I would have stopped to take pictures.

NV: Doo Lang Doo Lang Doo Lang...

SA: (Laughing) Yes! It's dangerous to notice this kaleidoscope of fractured information coming at us all day long.

CS: That brings me to another question. Several times in American Cockroach, the question is asked, "Are you God?"

NV: It's a good question to ask.

SA: God is a dangerous space alien who threatens us daily.

NV: We are on this rolling shit blue marble to suffer.

CS: Rock and roll seems to be a main character also, perhaps *the* main character in American Cockroach. Why did you make that decision?

NV: Musical notes map out our personal history and become a measure of all our moments as they grow into years. Music, like all art, is what affects the day.

SA: Through art we transcend. We're not defined by our circumstances. What do I have to do to get another absinthe in this joint?

NV: I'll take care of these white Christian niggers.

At this point we took a break. While Nick threatened the bartender with a pool cue in an attempt to get us more drinks, I disappeared down a labyrinth of stairs leading to the men's room. Coming back, I felt a little lightheaded, and at that moment I saw a cockroach dart across the hallway outside the bathroom. I'm just glad it didn't start talking to me. After the second round of drinks turned into the third and fourth round, the talk became even more informal. They mentioned the books they read while writing, the music they heard, the art they examined. Names were dropped. Terry Southern, Jean Cocteau, Marc Bolan, Wallace Berman, The Beatles, Elvis, of course, Thomas Pynchon, Jack Parsons, Lenny Bruce, the Comte de Lautréamont, and they always returned to Candy, God's pop star daughter.

All in all, it's my kind of book. American Cockroach is a satire of contemporary America inside a rock and roll novel. The authors left the Pig n' Whistle together, but Vukmanovich, still brandishing a pool cue, stopped just outside the door then staggered to the right where he leaned over and vomited into the backseat of a 1986 Blu Sofisticato Maserati double parked in front of the Egyptian Theatre. He should have fled the scene of the crime, but he became distracted by Dennis Hopper's star on the Hollywood Walk of Fame. Anderson noticed it too, said something about Rudyard Kipling then kept walking and, maybe I'd had too many cosmopolitans, but it seemed to me that she started to levitate and float away.

Cosmo Sostenuto
Hollywood, California
February 25, 2018

The Professor spoke of the Soul.

Transmigration.

Liquid Lou lit a joint.

Hot Darla snapped the waistband of her thong.

Black Charley clicked his boots.

Mad Henry beat on the desk with his fists.

Crazy Adam howled at the blackboard.

Blind Richard opened a warm beer.

Transvestite Tom pleaded for a strange erection.

Careless Cathy sang Sinatra a cappella.

And it was at that moment

Fabulous Frank

Pulled the green metal pin

From a vintage hand grenade.

And without letting go,

Time fused the Socratic myth.

ONE

I started early in the morning, really early. Six a.m. early.
I walked into this familiar Alabama stench and ordered a brown
long-neck. No glass was offered. A paisley stained rinsed out
tired old white woman with a croupier green eye-patch smirked
through black-brown broken teeth and disappeared back into
the kitchen of hard boiled eggs.

Hurricane Robert's thick rain pelted the hot tar scarred
roof. I could hear the echoing persistence of leaks, the stubborn
drip drip of a thousand dirty raindrops. I was alone. To the left
was a jukebox...one of those old half-moon glass uncommon
marvels from the fifties. It took quarters, American silver
quarters. It would not take those bastard Nixon quarters with
the copper jammed into the cold heart of Washington's off-
center. All the disks were vinyl, the lost 45's of my youth.
Hitting E7 turned on the hornpipe of another generation, that
mad, free time when Jimmy James sang his way out of the void
and into the Marquee Club in London.

Slowly spinning in cheap, black oiled boots, I felt that life
affirming secret sensation that lived in the silence between the
beats. That sophisticated slut perception of rhythm that only a
jaded whore experiences when her corrupt pleasure center
finally reaches the apex of her discontent.

"No dancing! No dancing allowed! I have no license for dancing. Stop dancing. Stop dancing, now!"

I turned toward the direction of the old woman's rant and smiled behind dark panes, still spinning in slow defiance.

"Stop! You must stop dancing. Can't you hear me? Stop! Stop now!"

I tossed my hands palms up in a shoulder high gesture of surrender.

Suddenly the bar door flew open, and in walked Nancy Masterson. My ex-fiancé was in her party clothes, a short blue jean skirt, black Givenchy thigh-high stockings and warehouse black heels. A frayed color block raglan tee and a cheap black leather jacket finished the look.

"Margaret stop screaming," she said, half laughing "Don't you know who you're screaming at?"

"It ain't Governor Wallace! And it ain't Jesus Christ! Tell that bastard to stop dancing!"

Masterson ordered a Budweiser, and I tilted the jukebox. She sauntered in my direction, cold drink in hand. Her bleached skin, her molasses curls and cracked virgin smile filled a morning hole in my memory. She touched my right cheek with the back of her cool hand and said "Hello, Billy." I could smell the memory of intimacy on her warm breath. Nancy Masterson was truly mad. Nuts. Crazy. No impulse control. No brakes. When she sat down, her skirt rose to ridiculous heights, revealing she was not wearing any panties. She had an ass that couldn't have been more of a delicacy if it'd been packed with caviar.

Four years ago on a ruthlessly hot summer afternoon in Irondale, Alabama, Ms. Masterson ransacked my checking account for sixty-five large and ran off to Hollywood in search of something. She found nothing. The west is not the best.

"I should knock you out."

"Billy, I can explain."

"You've been running for three years, sister."

"I called your mother."

I swallowed hard on the bottle and lit a cigarette. Masterson began to speak and I put tobacco stained fingers on her soft magenta lips.

"Do you have my money, honey?"

"I can see this was a mistake," she managed to say while I reached under the table, grabbed her by the waistband of her skirt and pulled her forward roughly into the Formica table top. Her expression seemed to register a combination of fear and sexual pleasure. I asked again for my money. She eyed me warily. "Give me my money or I'll strap you naked to the hood of the Chrysler."

"Billy Ball don't you dare."

"I'll drive you all the way to Mobile."

"Billy, stop!"

"Face down, so you can look at me through the windshield."

"Billy?"

"What?"

"I'll write you a check."

"I'm staying in town till it clears."

"Fine," she mumbled flatly while looking at the floor.

"And I'm staying with you."

She appeared to think long and hard about this, and then flashed her killer white smile.

"I have to go to the ladies room."

"You're not a lady," I laughed.

Masterson frowned and abruptly rose from her seat, turning toward the bathroom.

"I'm coming with you."

"Like hell you are," she protested.

"We'll see," I said firmly while I marched her to her destination.

"You're still a pervert, Billy Ball," she screamed, slamming the door behind her.

"Is there a window in there?" I asked the barkeep.

"Yeah, you gotta keep a close eye on that one," belched the old woman behind the bar. She exhaled, and a cloud of cigarette smoke engulfed her half toothless head in an opaque death shroud. She shook her head as if to free herself and coughed several times. I suddenly felt uneasy.

"Two more long necks." I flashed her the peace sign.

"She's a god damn grifter disguised as an undercover model. Knew her grandmother. Crazy factory slut. Married Birmingham rich. Had one daughter who was Miss Alabama in 1970. She gets knocked up by some minor league shortstop then squirts out that beautiful mess from her unholy thighs." I suppressed the urge to laugh at her baroque observation. "She's twenty-two, ain't never been married, and I don't know how many blind fetuses have been left on the side of the road."

"Don't you dare slander me, Margaret Sagecock," screamed the now eavesdropping Masterson.

"Hush your painted mouth, child."

"Masterson is a fine, fine southern name. What family doesn't have a mark on its shield?"

I escorted an even more disgruntled Nancy toward the front door. She turned her graceful head in the direction of her tormentor. "And what kind of name is Sagecock, huh, Margaret?"

"I'll wash your mouth out with soap you little slut."

"Oh hush, you old gray gash."

"Masterson, please," I pleaded while carrying the beers outside. Now we were out in the open air where she jumped into my arms and kissed me deeply. "I'll drive," she stated flatly, and we traveled north toward the Heights.

5

I am reminded that Masterson still appears to be sex personified as we shift into hallucinatory speeds in the black MGB.

"There's some coke in the glove box," she mentioned casually. It had stopped raining. I looked at her quizzically and declined. I was having enough difficulty keeping my pipe lit as the sleek convertible twisted high into the morning sky. She played Aja on the car stereo. She parlayed her 65k theft into close to a million. Twelve million confederate. Now she was prepared to pay me back for her misdeed, with interest. The wind blew through what was left of my longish hair, and the morning sun seemed to bake my sunglasses to my face in a perma seal of sweat. I was 20 years older than Nancy, though I didn't look or act the part. I thought of myself as one of those perpetually good looking bad boys, but in truth I hadn't grown up, I'd just grown older.

While drinking our perspiring bottles of cold beer, I turned to look at Masterson, appreciating her alluring beauty. "You're a heartbreaker." I was surprised that I'd said it out loud instead of thinking it. She adjusted her hands on the red leather steering wheel and did not smile. Her thighs were totally exposed to the tops of her opaque stockings. I slowly lowered my sunglasses to get a better view.

"Like what you see?" she asks. I said nothing. She apologized while shifting into second and sliding into a sharp left. Today, she has the reflexes of a race car driver. Her demeanor is confident and unruffled. This is foreplay for Nancy, I know this. Before we reach her house she'll orgasm on the hot leather bucket seat. For her, anything's a fetish. Anything. My stares, this car -- that's what'll do it today. While I stared, stoned, at her trampy pumps she shifted gears, brakes and accelerated. "You're making me hot, Billy," she quietly sighs, seemingly reading my thoughts. I sip from the long neck. "You need to be punished," I laughed. She downshifted into second, a killer S curve that folded out in front of her like an asphalt blossom. "Do you still drip during the end of Steve Gadd's drum solo?" I shamelessly inquired.

The speedometer raced toward eighty, the red needle of the tachometer erect and quivering. "I won't be a part of this," I said, mostly to myself. Abruptly, she double clutched from fourth to second and slammed on the brakes. Her magnificent hips became detached from the slick leather seat, her thin hands clamping onto the cherry leather wheel like a cat's claw, connected to the screaming brakes and wet angel thighs as she rode her cowgirl climax into a sharp right that segued into a 180 degree cessation. She exhaled, turned her adorable glowing face in my direction and quipped breathlessly, "Anybody ever tell you that you look like Donald Fagen?" I shook my head in amused disgust and climbed out of the low, sleek raven vehicle.

Moments later, I'm staring at a well maintained grey framed

contemporary nestled amongst pine. "Sixty-one." I stated. "No, fifty-eight," she corrects. Spilling the remainder of her beer onto the lawn, she declared "There's a surprise inside." "My money!" I snarled. "Why yes, that too, darling."

There are two walls of glass separated near the fifteen panel mahogany front door. Three multi-level smoking flat roofs extend across the skyline and the residence comes equipped with carport and garage adjacent to a stunningly blue indoor swimming pool. Upon entering, I'm impressed. An off-white couch and sofa in horizontal airport mode sit upon hardwood floors. I tilted my head while removing my sunglasses, exhaling in relief.

"You've done really well for yourself," I said. She's not listening. It's all coming back to me.

"Make yourself at home," and she disappeared behind a bleached door. Within seconds she sauntered back into the living room wearing a smoldering swimsuit. An aqua mist banded halter and matching Brazilian-cut bottom. "Bloody Mary?" she asked. This time I don't answer. She prepared two. "Lemon with yours?" The phone rings. She answers, curses, then hangs up. She turned the stereo on, pushed play. Variations on Sinister #3, a live Zappa guitar solo rips through the interior. She danced lightly on small bare feet. Her hair shook. Her hips shimmied. She trimmed the celery in rhythm with a stainless steel knife on a dry, dusty cutting board. The

8

morning sun cut blindly from above, the shaft of light intersecting her fumbling through a kitchen drawer for sunglasses. Child's eyewear. Strawberry Shortcake brand panes. The combination was breathless. She may have been the most beautiful woman in the red states. Right now. Right here. We ate some majoun and fell asleep in each other's arms. The next thing I knew, it was evening.

"I'm going for a swim," she abruptly stated. I didn't join her. Masterson stole my money and left me standing with my thumb up my ass at the justice of the peace. I remembered when I first met her years ago, a young girl running toward an ugly yellow school bus, her cheerleading outfit bouncing to reveal her red panty bottom. How old was she then, seventeen at the most? I pulled my shiny black '67 Chevrolet Corvette convertible slowly to the curb, my signature license plate seemed appropriate- "LHOOQ". The school bus doors closed and a huge puff of polluted black diesel covered the sun momentarily. It'd left without her; I'd heard her yell "Fuck!" I told her I'd get her to school and, after initially calling me an asshole and telling me to buzz off, she eventually relented and got in the car. After introductions, she asked me "What do you do?"

"I'm an artist."

"Ooh, an artist."

"Yeah, I paint pictures that nobody wants." We both

9

laughed.

"How do you afford this ride? It's really sweet by the way." She ran her manicured fingers across the dashboard.

"I won a football bet."

"Yeah right."

"No, really doll. I'm an investor."

"You're a gambler and a degenerate. You won this Corvette?"

"Yes. Guy bet me twelve dimes, couldn't pay so I got this car."

"What's a dime?" she asks.

"A thousand."

"What's five hundred?"

"A nickel."

"Hmm, I see. What do you call a hundred?"

"A buck."

"What do you call a dollar?"

"In God We Trust." We both laughed again.

I dropped her off that day and picked her up. Took her to a bookstore. Here we were, years later, and after Turkish coffee and sticky Lebanese pastries she presented me with a 3M bubble cushioned yellow mailer filled with one hundred thousand in large bills, all clean, all untraceable. My sixty-five plus thirty-five interest.

I'm not noticing. My coffee colored eyes are glued to an

ultramarine cake smear of magnificent pigment, a painting on linen. As large as a car hood. As powerful as a wizard. A sheet of pure American cool blue veneer. I lit a cigarette. My mouth turned in a sour twist and I proclaimed "I'm taking this Willis with me."

"You're not taking my Thornton Willis," she laughed. Her eyes make contact with mine, I exhaled again. I'm oblivious to her graphic bikini now, and her gold details, her hot short.

"You owe me."

She laughed. "No."

"What's it called?"

"I don't remember," she stated definitively.

"No." My eyes scanned the art decorated walls of her residence. A small Basquiat, but it's a color copy collage – weak. Worth 20K tops. A spectacular early Not Vital is a possibility.

"Take the Koons. You've always loved the Italian hump painting."

Looking past her I zeroed in on the three bars of fluorescent lighting illuminated at the far end of the hall. "I could possibly live with the Flavin," I laughed.

"You're a bastard, Billy. Take the Willis, I'm taking a bath." She switches on the radio and it's Tommy James and the Shondells, *Mony Mony*. Two minutes and fifty-two seconds of pure 1968 American bliss. She stops singing along, mimicking

11

the raw vocal and hand claps long enough to say "Pour me a glass of wine, prick. I'll be soaking." She disappeared into the purple shadows of her home. *"Don't stop now come on Mony..."*

I poured two fresh glasses of burgundy, knocked as I entered her master bath, not waiting for permission to enter. The room was illuminated with a six stanchion platinum candelabra. There she was, floating amongst a white sea of *Mister Bubble,* slowly smoking an ultra-light and dropping the ashes onto an antique saucer. I sat on the floor while we both quietly sipped our wine. The elegance of John Coltrane's tenor sax drifted from the transistor radio like a fog. She smelled wonderful, a queen bee in her hive surrounded by her sacred objects and curiosities. There were white roses bathing in two translucent indigo vases. The far wall presented a hermetically sealed copy of *Never Mind the Bollocks, Here's The Sex Pistols* signed by Cook, Jones, Rotten and Vicious. A tiny black and white television glowed silently next to an aluminum heavy metal blue *Easton* baseball bat that gleamed within arms' reach of the hot water faucet. A pair of white pantyhose, newly washed, dripped from a marble towel rack onto several water-stained copies of *Architectural Digest.* Coral satin pajamas were draped over a silver curtain rod, shed like forgotten skin. Fresh green apples on the marble counter top, and a seductive assemblage of ankle strap sandals and cut-out stilettos littered the corner. She's still a Southern American Princess. Eyes of electric black. She speaks first.

"Shave my legs, Billy," she giggled. "I'm too ripped."

"I can't see."

She flopped her leg over the edge of the tub like a petulant child. "Come on, shave me."

I reached for the double edged razor and lightly drew it along the length of her gam. Top and bottom. Then it's the right leg, rinse and repeat. She stood.

"Do my thighs."

"Is that a double entendre?" I couldn't resist.

"Yes, and I knew you'd say that."

I'd been here before. I knew every fold, mark and blemish of this world map that was her body-the tributaries, the oceans, mountains and valleys. She receded into the tub water to the top of her chin, her hair splayed out around her head like a halo, ghostly tendrils of soap swirling away from her holy relic face. I wiped my fingers on a small white hand towel while she turned the hot water tap with her mauve painted toes. The full moon's reflection shined back at us from the glistening black and white tile floor.

"I wish I was Elizabeth Taylor," she whispered.

"Would I be Nicky Hilton or Burton?"

She does not answer. Rhetorical questions don't require response. Too bad. She continued. "When I was seventeen, you bought me my first pair of high heels. They made me look six-four. You said they were magic shoes. You were my mentor. I always came back to you. I went to college and acted like a university slut. You asked me if you could watch. You taught me art and music and vice. We read books aloud to each other. Painted pictures together. Ate quaaludes. But you always took me back when I was naughty. Always." She turned to face me. "Shampoo my hair, please." She turned her back and tilted her head down, her long neck turned with the grace of a renaissance painting. I gently piled her hair into a shampoo turban. She spoke with her eyes closed, a side-effect of the sensory pleasure my touch brought her, triggering another flood of memory. "We could live like this again. You can bathe me, hold me, scold me," she giggled. "I can give you sons, handsome ones." She continued, her voice barely audible. "I can give you a son named Jackson. I could be Rosa Luxemburg or Frances Farmer. When I went for my master in business, you raped my ears with Don Van Vliet, but that cacophony transformed into a sound I'd later crave. During my master program I registered for an advanced statistics course I didn't have the prerequisites to take based on my bachelors in art history. 'Unqualified', they said. If it was that hard, no one could do it, I told them. I can do hard things, Billy. My aunt wrote the eulogy they read at my father's funeral. She didn't have the strength to read it aloud, but she had the power to write those enormous words. That's the first time I felt my heart breaking, but I realized it was necessary. It was necessary because my heart had to break to expand to an equally enormous size. It needed that expanded containment to have the space required to live in a world where such beautiful words had been spoken. I shed that exoskeleton and grew, and I can do it again. You played a trumpet, badly, as my apartment burned down."

"You were the Princess of Tuscaloosa," I managed to say, my voice cracking under the weight of remembrance. Suddenly a car horn blows twice from outside, breaking the spell.

"What, Billy?"

"Let's rinse your hair. I have to go."

"Please Billy."

"No, I can't."

The sharp alarm of the driver's horn broke off the conversation. She gulps some wine, shampoo suds dancing on her eyelashes. "Tell him to go away," she slurred.

"I can't, Nancy."

"You never call me Nancy."

"Masterson!"

"What?" She started to cry, and the horn bellowed again like the answer to a question she never asked. "Give me two hours, I just need two hours."

"Goodnight, Masterson."

"No, Billy." She reached out to me, her face contorted by hot tears. "I promise to be good."

I was out of there. I snapped into action, removing a psycho/social angst ridden monochromatic oil stick portrait by Elliot Miller, an American painter of mimetic contours suggesting heterosexual acts of indecency evoking holy iconography. I could live with this painting. The small cheap drop cloth canvas still reeked of the oral and satanic, figures on the far right enjoying the unholy sensation of infidels floating on a cloud of bacon and anus bouquet. Faceless whores and disembodied penis arms salute the rear entry of Hades, oral ecstasy drug ejaculation cohabitating with the hovering pink orgasm of a flying bird. I removed it from the wall, grabbed my envelope of cash with the other hand, then out the door in seconds headed for a faded white cab under the spotlight of the moon.

"Good evening," I said to the driver. "Get me off this fucking hill."

"Where we goin mon?" asked the Rasta driver.

"Birmingham 8th Avenue Café." Located paradoxically on Third Street.

"Yeah mon, you go from mountain to trenchtown, seen." I laughed; relieved to be in the musty, forgotten place that was the inside of this cab. We roared out of the driveway, incense burning on the dash in an unspoken apology for the smell. A small, smeared photograph of Haile Selassie framed in gold paper hung from the cigarette lighter. A beat up silver boom

16

box sat on the front passenger seat secured by a beige tattered seatbelt. Clever. But there was no music. The late night drone of sports radio became aural white noise as we descended down into the fog and gloaming. We didn't speak, thankfully. I left a handsome gratuity, and then headed for that vulgar pack of lies that is *The National Gallery of Art*.

TWO

Location: Georgetown, Maryland. I drove the tidy fall streets of one of my favorite cities, illegally drinking a six-pack with the late John Lennon unleashing some primal scream through the car speakers. I usually preferred the company of recorded music as opposed to human beings, which likely makes me a misanthrope. Just slow riding, not thinking of Wittgenstein, which I sometimes do in these moments, looking at the hard female bottoms instead clad in straining denim containment. Beautiful, angelic blond college brats scurrying down and around cobblestone sidewalks, and I'm looking for a place to park the New Yorker. I made a lazy turn onto Federal Place, noticing two black haired and light yellow skinned oriental girls sitting on concrete steps, legs held apart with school texts. I'm reminded of fragile porcelain dolls. There is no place to park... I decided to park in a private drive. I wrap a white handkerchief on the antenna and leave a bogus note of explanation on the windshield...*Went to call a tow truck!* I hoped these rich hog bastards had a sense of humor.

I walked about seven self-assured blocks in no particular direction when I came upon a gothic Catholic cathedral. A few slow people dragged their feet as they exit the sanctuary including a small well-dressed boy child, a grey woman sporting three hundred dollar Karan flats, one prematurely balding homoerotic, an old negro witch with bulging varicose veins mapped on her legs like roads to nowhere hanging onto her equally unstable Puerto Rican meal ticket...people united in common superstition.

I decided to go inside, maybe change my luck, because my luck was lost. I had dropped three dimes on several football games with an offshore account. Cayman Islands. And my plastic bank was close to maxed, also grandfather Ford passed into the void while watching a black and white porno flick from the early sixties. Bad timing. And there were several outstanding warrants waiting for me back in the collapsed cinema of my youth, the obscene and invisible hazy, dark, illogically cold and filthy confluence of Pittsburgh, PA.

I walked into the church with the latest USA Today football line firmly gripped in my left hand. Your God hates the left hand. It's the magic hand I saw in a dream. *In the dream I was attending an estate auction, digging through crates of vinyl records. That's when I saw an album by a recording artist – shit; I thought I had all his records! – this one's called "Mindfuck." The cover had the magic left hand attached to an arm, attached to a face that wore a mask with an obscenely long nose menacing an opening in a human skull. The magic left hand.* It was one of those dreams where I woke up and remembered it all, sketched it and painted this album cover that never existed. The day I exhibited the painting, that same artist died in a house fire. I never again showed the painting to anyone. I should have known it was an omen. The dream. *An estate auction.* Pay attention to the signs from now on, I told myself.

It's velvet dark inside...I smelled death...I smelled destruction while I lifted all the major coins from the donation boxes. I noticed the red glaring bulb of the confessional beckoning not unlike some filthy hot whore house in New Orleans. I entered the sweaty guilt enclosure and said all of the obligatory bullshit that I learned from watching American television. And then he spoke. A faint swish voice from the other side of the comic confessional. It was the breathless scree scree screech of a fidgety, nervous, delicate and flustered flour sack of human shit. Thirty-five years ago in the borough of Ataraxia I swore to the Dove that I would never ever forget that debased, indecent vomit voice...Father McCartney. This pig of a pastor was a felon. An unconvicted molester set free with gold Pope bounty lawyers.

"Tell me, son, when was your last confession?"

"I've never had the urge to confess...you holy geek freak...goat fucking bastard." I lost it, predictably. Didn't even finish my spit spewing rant when I drove both my fists and head through the flimsy screen partition. I grabbed that slow shocked bastard by the black lapels and yanked him through the splintered opening. I wrenched that yellow Yankee until his pathetic head and obese torso came clean and clear, but his greasy hips were too bulky for me to complete the assault. It was him. Christ, I've lost it.

I bolted out of the box, knocking the door loose from its hinge. No thought here. I smashed and kicked my way into his holy chamber and whipped his stuck ass until he went cold. One last blow to his balding skullcap and my hands went blood ink. I ripped the wallet from his fat right hip pocket and helped myself to six hundred dollars.

I slipped on several hundred rosary beads as I exited; no one was alarmed or even seemed to notice. I told myself, walk slowly! I went to the nearest graffiti molested phone booth and reported my car stolen. The police were sympathetic. They were in possession of the New Yorker. No tow charges.

At the station house I casually spoke with Officer Nelson, a failed aesthete turned centurion. "One other thing, officer," I said, "Have you ever noticed that when you look into a mirror everything is, well, backwards? You know, a mirror image. Does that mean we view ourselves in error? If so, if this is dogmatic, then what is the point of narcissism? How could we fall in love with our own image if said image is a mistake? A deviation? An inaccuracy of monster lapse and proportion? I believe Kandinsky said that the mirror image was not human." Nelson had a look of narco-analysis written across his cold, puzzled face. He didn't answer.

I headed for Johnstown. The War Memorial Arena. I'm going to hear The Texas School Book Depository...a neo-punk band comprised of the offspring and descendants of political assassins. Too true.

THREE

Your God, the band was a horrendous electronic embarrassment. The audience became one in collective hate. An array of objects – shoes, umbrellas, and an empty half-pint bottle—flew in a unified critique toward the musicians. The Texas School Book Depository was name dropping during their slowed down punk rock raga about death.

John Coltrane is dead.

Miles Davis is deceased.

Charlie Parker is expired.

Chet Baker is departed.

Thelonious Monk is perished.

Charles Mingus is late.

Bud Powell is no more.

Dick Twardzik is resting in peace.

Dizzy Gillespie is gone.

Benny Goodman is done for.

Duke Ellington is lifeless.

Count Basie is no longer.

Bix Beiderbecke is defunct.

Tommy Dorsey is snuffed out.

Coleman Hawkins is pushing up daisies.

Billie Holiday is gone by the board.

Harry James is liquidated.

Gene Krupa is inanimate.

Scott Joplin is erased.

Glenn Miller is with his maker.

Red Nichols is gone to his reward.

Bessie Smith is parted.

Mel Torme is extinct.

Lester Young is the way of all flesh.

But my fucking neighbor.

He still breathes.

I was one of the first to exit. One hour into the night's farewell, soaring through the indigo blue black mountains of western Pennsylvania...red flashing lights blinded the rearview mirror. The green glow of the dashboard read, at a quick glance, ninety-seven miles per hour. God damn mother fuck! I'd been clocked by a Pennsylvania State Trooper.

I casually rolled down the electric window, then fished around in the glove box for registration, insurance card...I noticed that my Smith and Wesson thirty-eight caliber Police Chief's Special was fully loaded and, with my luck, in violation of at least seventeen gun laws. A stainless steel walnut handled cannon. I placed it strategically on the front red leather seat and cover it with a Polo USA flag sweater. I located my driver's license and waited.

The side mirror was klieg lit. I noticed that the trooper was a wide, towering black man dressed as a state cop. I thought of Halloween, he's not believable in this role. He ambled up to the car, smiling down at my license offered willingly. There's something suspect, and while still smiling at my identification he said "I would like to search your vehicle, Mr. Ball."

"I, ah, would rather you didn't and just write out your summons so I can..."

"Listen, Mr. Ball." He quickly recited a terse script now. "I would hope for your sake you would cooperate. Now if you'll please exit the vehicle." He opened the door and bent his arm back, reaching for his revolver.

"Look, whatever you find is going to be thrown out of court because I have refused to give you permission to search this vehicle."

"GET OUT OF THE CAR NOW," he screamed and, with the jolt of that command my foot slipped off the brake and the other overcompensated by hitting the accelerator. He'd already walked to the trunk, gun pointed and I felt the crush of flesh and bone as I rolled over his bulk. I was completely behind him, and my headlights hit the wreckage of his body. In that spotlight, I noticed his ugly bulging yellow eyes turning death red in their sockets. Spit ran down onto his slick, shaved double chin. Steam rose like smoke over pools of blood that slowly formed around his now inanimate body.

I panicked. Before anything else could happen, I grabbed the thirty-eight and with my right arm extended I fired. One shot, then BAPBAP. One shot in the ear, one through his stout, round throat, and the third blew his left orbit through the back of his brain. The look on his face as he lay on pavement assured me I would have no more trouble with this one.

I got out slowly, my mind catching up with the quick horror of events. "Remove the video tape from his cruiser," some split part of my identity said back to me. Replaced the Chrysler's license plate with one of several I had in the trunk. This did not happen. Now what? I stared down at the steaming pile of fresh corpse and, with my handkerchief, I remove a Monopoly *Get Out Of Jail Free* card from my wallet and lodge it into his inanimate oozing lips. My neighbors live next door to a spree killer, don't even know it. I'm headed for a rendezvous with the McCoy twins from Brewton, West Virginia.

FOUR

It feels like nine below zero inside the car as I jet through mountain clouds of the Keystone state toward the cool sadness of the lost Virginia. I feel like Alvin Lee. Bringing it all back home. The shameless guitar notes' low vibrations push on the windows accompanied by my own high tinnitus ringing in my ears.

Again the psycho-television. The last capitalist battle, the assault, the bloodshed will level every motherfucking money changer who ever flew ninety-five miles per hour across the holiest of blacktop black like a priest's robe and equally indifferent.

It was the summer of '68
He walked into the Greentree Holiday Inn
There were five whites sitting at the bar
Long manes of fur cascaded madly
He asked the bartender
"Who are those spinning tops?"
"That's Mitch Ryder
And the Detroit Wheels."

From Vegas to Baker Street...the cool calm carnage will reek with yellow Ono star bursts of red rabid menstruation. Brown hair, white teeth and black lipstick. Hole's Black Lipstick Lesbian Tour smeared onto fake holy robes of inhibition...the champion gene pool crumbles into a heap of protestant howl. Stop.

Television, the mimetic bastard child, will axe its first negro clone born, the cathode ray moonlet head chews its lost parent while flesh defecating ghosts of Microsoft awareness spew the bloody bark of nature back upon its mother...the blue whore of video. No survivors here. The stinking black diesel left this last dance with a guitar strapped to the farthest sun of his own making, at the crossroads with Robert Johnson and the devil, the Goat God long gone. The deal played without divinity, no smirking omnipresence shaking his mistake of a head in the new direction of his error, unable to escape the greasy mess of his own spirit.

Three bleak black Americans were the last to go. Some strange and pathetic holy ghost encased in skulls of Lincoln. Some raw racist digital abomination. The three screamed pathetic Wallace fuel into the absent mouth of Texas Oswald prophecy. There was no fascination in their grab government eyes, no saint of the polygraph. Pointing due North from their crossroad perpendicular, East was homophobic, West homoerotic and South just homogenized. The obsessed October of their youth shook with white sidewalls and Indian summer transformed into a meandering hunting season. The explosion, the very last exact hollow bomb of Malcolm exaggeration created a grey radio wave devoid of hue.

I found myself in a lost, gone tavern six miles outside of Brewton chain smoking cigarettes and drinking domestic draft.

The barmaid was uneducated and undone, sporting half-ripped t-shirt and silver G string matched with obligatory scarred and scuffed high heel pumps, once white. She was a skinny illiterate unfortunate with matching blue purple bruises on her arm and thigh. I imagined she was one of those young whores making extra cash gulping blow jobs in the back of her mother's Oldsmobile convertible. One of those fractured females who may have believed, ten years ago, that Axl Rose was Jesus Christ. I finished my beer and tipped five dollars, she seemed shocked and grateful.

I turned the Chrysler onto route twenty-four and headed northwest for six looping miles toward Brewton. The McCoy twins were lounging in front of their robin's egg blue mobile home, sitting and splashing in a child's fill-er-up swimming pool. They appeared stoned and drunk. Twins Alice and Mary, matching recessive genes. The egg split and left them there, turned into golden West Virginian mermaids, their warm breath laced with cold beer. Sirens who'd already hit the rocks, the song long ended. They tossed empty cans of Budweiser as the New Yorker creeped to a halt.

"Well if it ain't."

"Billy, big dick."

"BALL!" They both belch in unison.

"Ain't that the fawkin' impotent Ball brother."

"No, no that's the BIG COCK BALL BROTHER, the

young one."

"The psycho-bastard child?"

"That's the one." They both started to hoot and then laugh.

Road fatigue leaves me without patience or humor. "Shut the fuck up you sick, twisted lesbians."

"Now Billy, that ain't no way to talk to yer sisters."

"We ain't never sucked no pussy like you Billy."

"You ain't no Ball sisters, just ball busters. Now come over here and give me a hug. Don't make me strip search you two!"

"Oh Billy!"

After three days of drunken madness, that following morning, Tuesday, the girls dropped a bomb into my psyche. I had sensed that something was not quite right. The twins were mad sex witches. A coven of two, they were into everything including hot colored wax, toys, you name it, and things you didn't have a name for and never would. Alice spoke for both of them. She was the oldest of perfect identical twin angels by three minutes.

"Billy, we have something to tell you and nothing you say or do is going to change our minds so, here goes…ah. We are…"

"We're done." said Mary.

"Yes and we're checking out of this hotel."

"Together. Today. Understand?" asked Mary.

I became sick to my stomach as I stared into their absent

faces with matching lost blue eyes, misplaced blond strands of hair. I tried to reason with them. I threatened them. They laughed. They had no regrets, no persuasion and no reflection or argument was going to change their destiny.

The trailer park was white noise silent. The hum of several air conditioners. The whore roar of a dual exhaust. The signal that it was too late.

I watched them both enter their father's dark green sixty-seven Pontiac LeMans and Alice shot Mary...POP...then Alice shot herself...POP.

FIVE

The nether world, where the sinning dead continue to exist, and if the damned do suffer everlasting punishment, torment and destruction then it'll be served up with an American capitalist grin.

The township was dark and cold, the Chrysler crunched over frozen leaves and I was close to my roots...the West Hills. I killed the lights and the engine and collapsed on the front seat. I had...had enough of gambling, violence, murder, dope...and mind disease, and murder-suicide. I passed out in the car in front of my sister's house. A cold yellow sun bore through bent sunglasses. Diane and I embraced. She removed her house key from her chain and I watched her scrawny ass disappear.

I walked into Diane's house feeling like a pathogenic bacteria invading a sterile environment. Mutated, resistant to antibiotics. I was anathema to these sterile, black and sanitized square rooms. My sister must be fucking Mr. Clean.

I decided to have breakfast as I showered. I grabbed a half-gallon plastic container of orange juice from the refrigerator, an unopened green plastic wrapped wedge of Frigo Parmesan cheese, and a half empty jar of Vlasic mild yellow pepper chunks. I'm going to pay for this self-abuse. It's the kind of morning that would send Bob Evans into a prolonged state of projectile vomiting, and all his aged clientele gagging on their omelets in God's Formica waiting room.

On very special mornings such as these, when I am too tired, wrecked or hung over to shower properly, I'll place a wooden folding chair in the shower stall and let the water flush down upon me in a pathetic sitting position. You can do anything in this manner. Eat, read, smoke, shower, masturbate, shit and puke if you choose. I learned this technique from a brain damaged Vietnam veteran. My father, Frank.

It took a half-hour to wash the residual filth from my skin... I watched tiny pieces of parmesan drown in a water vortex of shampoo, loose hair and soap scum. CLEAN. Well, clean enough. I wrapped my sister's light white 100% cotton bathrobe around my aching frame and slept for eight hours in her bedroom.

I thought of Alice and Mary McCoy. I have no guilt about the trooper or the priest. I stayed in Pittsburgh just long enough to get out. Headed for Boston and all points north. I got lucky. Fell into a couple of thousand the hard way. U. Mass plus three. I loaded the Chrysler with two hundred cassettes and one hundred and forty-four bottles of beer, Heineken. Six pairs of black jeans and an assortment of black sweaters...ivory black, mars black, Clemente black, coal black, night black, jet black, Xerox black and bottomless black...a used seven hundred dollar coffee black long rider coat and a pair of thirty-eight dollar flat black oiled boots from Walmart.

It took seven hours to reach the New York state line. A couple of hours later I eased the Fifth Avenue within acceptable glide speed, entering Connecticut. Those smiling badges are real bastards. Four hours later, Fenway Park is on my right and within seconds I'm cemented into the unforgiving gridlock of Boston traffic.

The mind becomes strawberry Jell-O. Imagine some fur-draped rinsed out brunette flipping the finger from her silver Bavarian Motor Work, or the Vaseline flash brown Mexican, or the flamboyant, slippery Puerto Rican cutting you off at the Callahan tube, or maybe it's the poor off-white Italian with her mud smeared red galoshes jacking her Venezuelan as her cum stained yellow Honda Civic cuts and bends across three lanes of congested traffic on her way to the free V.D. clinic. It's full fool moon madness. It's a blueblood cowboy blitzkrieg, it's cruising bloody Mary secretaries or the blond coast guard reserve crew cut with snake cavity smile.

I never drive around in this city without some protection. Along with the Model Sixty Police Chief's Special, I've been known to brandish a brick, a pipe, or a Willie Stargell autographed baseball bat. This evening, protection came wrapped as a black handled construction hammer. I only had to reach for it once as I headed for America's Sodom and Gomorrah, Chelsea, Massachusetts.

SIX

It'd been snowing for the past couple of hours, there had to be twelve inches, maybe eighteen in some places. The Tobin Bridge appeared haunted and evil, a dirty massive steel structure that tore the heart out of a once respectable town, Chelsea by the Sea.

I turned right onto Cary Avenue and came bumper to bumper with an egg yellow oriental driving a red Ferrari. We were face to face, I in the Fifth Avenue, he in his spaghetti ride. I could tell he was ripped on something, probably inhalant. There was only room for one vehicle to egress because of the plowed snow and the avenue's configuration. It was a RED STALEMATE. I had been driving eleven hours and my journey was white snow yards away from completion. Your God is dead! I flicked the high beams at him twice. He squinted and covered his eyes...I noticed long fingernails that glisten with polish...no response. Flashing the projected eye irritant again and again and again got him pissed. Finally he flashed prolonged high beams in my direction and blew his horn. I kept provoking him while he ranted, his red face exploding with anger behind the steering wheel while creeping his vehicle in a threat lunge stop. I twisted my mouth in a Kabuki grimace reminiscent of the Three Stooges and lowered the electric window, tossed my cowboy cigarette onto the hood of his car while waving my black hammer in his direction. Like Moe Howard, I'm more slapstick than rage, more of an escapee from the Massachusetts Behavioral Institute.

His passenger door swung open. I could see the little bastard and hear him cursing me in broken English in a rapid fire fury as he approached my car with a sword. At that moment I cranked the car stereo volume to deafening waves of distorted sound and pointed the Smith and Wesson right at his stoned eyes. Year of the moron! I opened the door and three empty Heineken bottles clattered down to the pavement like they'd rather escape, too. Moving slowly out of the car, I had the stainless steel head remover locked onto his twitching eyebrows. In my peripheral vision I saw an old man shoveling snow, his balding nosey wife chain smoking on a cold wooden porch. Time stopped—us two, Billy and this adversary. We were trapped in amber in this frozen moment, two carbon based life forms full of chemicals and bad ideas, locked in a combat that seemed more inevitable than any simultaneous event occurring at that moment—the jewelry store robbery 150 miles north, a window washer's scaffold tipping from the top of a high rise 30 miles east sending cleaning fluid mixed with dirt down to the pavement where it would cause a car to collide into a light pole, the loading dock of a warehouse 5 miles north where a truck, with electronics in stacked boxes, already marked as "received" by the shipping department, disappeared in that alley on the flatbed of an accomplice, a bank executive laundering money three blocks south—what's another disaster? Add it to the bouquet of terrible, misguided events, square city block blurry pixels that, seen from a distance, take shape. A patterned aerial grid picture emerging of just another day in the United States of America.

Time thawed and slowly lunged forward on my command. "That's right motherfucker, put that fucking sword down and get down on your Jap fuckin' knees." Slowly backing toward his car, the thick molasses of time frozen then melting gave him that slow, steady resolve.

"I sorry, I so sorry, I move car now."

"Drop that fucking sword you asshole!"

"I can't find Tobin Bridge. I look for Tobin, but I lost."

"You cocksuckers didn't have any trouble finding Pearl Harbor!"

His eyes lit up like Nagasaki when he heard my racist refrain, then the sonic low rumble detonation of his car in reversed gear followed by screeching tires exiting the scene. I never got the sword. I pulled the Chrysler into the vacated parking slot and went to see my cousin. The man with the shovel and his ugly chain smoking old cunt stared in disbelief, though the spell had been broken.

"Good evening," I said to both of them.

I opened the door to the vestibule and began to climb the

stained carpeted stairs and then the unconscious CLICK. *Burroughs is dead and so is language...the disappearance of the word is inevitable...long live the screenager. Slang, epithets, misguided ideas...it's a contributing factor to the decline of western civilization. The long ride down. Guevara was right...Gates will buy Cuba from Castro for eighty billion...Cuba was a forest of tropical cedar and mahogany long ago, you'll find it all rendered into fine furniture somewhere in Spain...and there will be an Oswald theme park...Fidel ends up with the corpse with no hands...and John Brisker rises, finally, in Uganda. The window shade is stained and cracked from the heat of the sun...there are no clean curtains...there are no dead drapes at all...the croupier says rock and roll is expired...he is right...pop music has become a lime green brain dead transmission of female punk phlegm. Rock clings vainly to its lewd life support system. Roll threatens to disengage the spinning magnets of Tesla's dream. Egyptian whore off pink pancake masks...bargain their raised skirts to reveal hot pink fishnet thigh-highs...immaculate synthetic nylon stretched across recently shaved ham and bone while the crack white palm of the mushroom man spanks a red vision into the distress of her embarrassed bottom...oh baby baby baby echoes across cheap motel carpet as the assault orgasm flames away, are you the one I've always loved? The song creeps into the ears of women staring at blouses on clothing racks in a department store, the subliminal marriage of the song lyrics locked to the price tag, a million consumer love matches.*

Americans are so fucking stupid...what a pathetic Republic...late capitalism has run amok. When we die we become star material, star matter...I do not believe you. Maybe that Teutonic psycho angel Nietzsche was right. FREE YOURSELF FROM YOURSELF. I never met that suicide Cobain, or Kerouac, or Cassady, or Dean, or Presley, or Morrison, or Piaf, or Clemente, or Van Gogh, or Pollock, or de Kooning, or that fuck Warhol, or Celine, or Camus, or the Pilate, or that whore master Kennedy, or Oswald, or Garbo, or the Virgin, but I did meet you.

SEVEN

My cousin left a note taped to her front door. "Went to Cape Cod, be back in a week...enjoy the apartment and say hello to my neighbor, Veronica Jewell."

The next two days I drank, relaxed and didn't venture out into Chelsea. On Friday, that adorable Jewell—I took her to see a movie, headed to the local Blanchard's for beer and cognac, drove to Revere Beach. We huddled under a camouflage blanket, got high and laughed. Veronica Jewell, five feet eight inches tall, black hair, black eyes, stacked. A real boozer. I liked her immediately.

"No one calls me Jewell, all my friends call me Veronica."

"I don't believe in the concept of friendship...if you don't mind...ah...I'll call you Jewell."

"I don't mind."

She seemed puzzled by this strange stance with regard to fellowship, and the crock of brown, hot steaming dog shit that it always has been. I did not expound.

"OK, then tell me, Billy, how do you make a living?"

"I invest in professional sports...and rob graves...big time graves...I guess that makes me a big time grave robber."

She laughed, cognac running out of the corners of her painted mouth onto her short dark green jacket.

"You are truly," she laughed, "truly full of shit."

"Would you like to hear about the Graceland Heist?"

"Ohhh, the Graceland Heist! Is this the Graceland in Memphis?" again she laughed, incredulous and so far unimpressed.

"Forget it. Let's have another shot."

"No, please continue. I'm sorry. I actually can't wait to hear this BULLSHIT!"

"I went to the mansion; the contraband was to be sold to an oriental consortium. Big dollars all around, millions actually."

She had this smile on her face, one of those piano keyboard smiles, uniform white keys glistening brilliantly. She sat back down and I opened two Heinekens.

I took a long drink from my cold green import, swallow, take another and tell her about the Tennessee larceny.

EIGHT DAYS AFTER THE FIFTEENTH ANNIVERSARY OF ELVIS' DEATH I was holed up in a Memphis Howard Johnsons with a seventeen year old crack addicted delinquent. I picked him up just off the interstate at a rest stop. He said his name was Diamond Dog. His parents named him after a David Bowie album. He told me to call him "Dog." I called him Morrison Clown. Quite a likable long-haired youth with a psycho fixation on Trent Reznor and Nine Inch Nails. He wore a Charles Manson Wheaties Box t-shirt and pair of off white stolen tuxedo slacks. He told me a fascinating story about the shoes he was wearing. Apparently he stole them off of one of the drunken offspring of J. Paul Getty. It was in San Francisco. There he was, passed out in front of PlumpJacks Wines & Spirits in the marina, a joint venture of the Getty family and the Newsomes. Dog lifted four thousand large bills and a pair of Bob Cousy autographed canvas high-tops while the old money faces of Fillmore Street looked on placidly from their wine tasting, nothing to do in the middle of the day but register mild alarm and some whispering at a crime in progress. They have not made that model of high-tops since that Texan pig Johnson was President. A real find, I told my young companion.

In Memphis, we checked out Graceland. We go on the Mansion Tour. Taking notes all the time about spatial relationships of the security system and exits. It was a WESTEC laser enhanced video scanning nightmare. Way out of my league. We would need the help of a professional. I decided to place a help wanted ad in the local Memphis Gazette. *Security Systems Expert Needed.* Act like I was requesting a bid for services for a chain of hotels. Immediate employment, consultation regarding high tech bank vaults, lasers, video surveillance, etc.

There wasn't much response. Your Christ, we were working out of a HoJo, limited resources to say the least. We had maybe five applicants, not promising until, like mad magic, an unemployed negro security expert appeared. On parole because of a botched diamond heist, he knocked on the motel door at seven o' clock on a Tuesday morning. I laid the cards on the table and the brother fell out.

"You must be one CRAZY white motherfucker. You want to steal the white cracker bones of Elvis Presley? This is some kind of joke, right? You crazy white fucks ain't serious. Are you?"

The Dog tossed thirteen hundred on the cheap laminated writing desk, and Calvin Washington looked at the money in disbelief.

"You honks are killing me. You can't be serious. You motherfuckers are out of your minds, this is bullshit."

The Dog threw five hundred more on the desk.

"You in or not, Ho?"

I told you Dog was not too bright, calling a black convicted felon a "Ho" was a bizarre bargaining tactic. The Dog pulled a knife; Calvin ripped the phone out of the wall. Things were off to a shaky start.

I stood between them and held out the eighteen hundred for Calvin's acceptance.

"Last chance MR. WASHINGTON."

Calvin took the green American dollars and I walked him to his truck. We talk. He agrees on the date.

The biggest heist in the downward sloping trajectory of western civilization is about to take place.

Like A Telltale Dream

Masterson returned today from the east coast. It was the year 2525. They dined on blue whale fetuses and white rice. Wine was illegal and considered a poison. Oral sex was outlawed and man was a slave to woman.

A TV over the restaurant's bar featured a documentary. Contemporary American History and the Hierarchy Within the Ruling Women: Red, Black Yellow Brown and White races, in that order. The DNA of the American Indian Female was considered holy. Men were genetically engineered and lived in strict behavioral environments, and women no longer suffered the indignity of menstruation.

Chewing on her whale and rice, Masterton laughed a full-mouthed muffled laugh at the clinical voice of the narrator as the camera panned through a cityscape at night, settling on the lit rectangle of an apartment window. Two silhouettes within.

"I should spank you and make you eat your own sperm," declared the Blood Queen.

"Whatever her Majesty wishes."

"Don't get impertinent with me, you piece of dog shit, you Man."

Immediately the handsome young stud apologized to his Queen and instantly took his life with a syringe of Dr. Jack's Instant

Heart Attack.

It was the year 2525, and this segment ended, predictably segueing into a commercial for Dr. Jack's Instant Heart Attack. Standing in a meadow, distorted smiling faces held up bottles of clear liquid death in dappled sunlight. When the series returned, a film montage and the unenthused narrator described the common sight of pathetic men on their knees servicing the superior sex in public. Erections are controlled electronically within the female brain. Man was reduced to a slurping dog ages ago. God returned to the Earth with his daughter, Candy, in the year 2222. She had a number one hit with her pop anthem Your God Loves the Color Red. Then the corresponding music video. "Admit it, he lives in your head," she sang through a menacing smirk while synchronized dancers spun around Christgirl like electrons orbiting her nucleus. The deep toned voiceover explains, as the video concludes, that sex between men in these 164 states is illegal whereas women, on the other hand, are encouraged to partake in lesbian affairs. Meet the New Strap-On Queen, Candy's latest hit video, plays during this segment. Product placement chorus girls wear the Strap-On Queen for Candy's dildo franchise, synchronized leg kicks displaying a perfect line of phalluses in varying hues.

It's eleven degrees out. Chance of snow flurries. No accumulation. More news and weather at 11:00.

Cold Monday Morning:

"She's got the sweetest tasting pussy on the planet."   Billy was not exaggerating.   It was documented in the High Court of her Majesty.

"Let's get a drink," said the twenty year-old, or was she?

"You're underage."

"I've got fake identification for thirty eight states, including Alaska."

Masterson refused to attend any family function that banned cigarette smoking.   She imagined a scenario involving Van Gogh and his pipe, and how she chose the mad artist, in a huff, over her immediate relatives.   "That's surreal."

"Piss, shit and blood…the rest is illusion."

Most of the professional football teams in the National Football League laid down and died like the corrupt dogs they are.   Six mad white men leapt to their deaths from hotel rooms in the screaming night desert of Nevada.   More news at 6:00.

It was New Year's Eve, and although there was little money, Masterson and her new lover purchased shell fish, red cigarettes and white table wine.   She was dating a very handsome young man she met in a book store; Andrew was a college student at the University, majoring in psychology.   They spent the evening at Olivia's residence, cooking dinner and seated around a huge dining room table.   Just the two of them.   She looked elegant, her straight red hair cut at an angle accentuating her pronounced cheekbones, black turtleneck sweater with black leather skirt and opaque nude stockings matched with comfortable flat black shoes. She never left Drew's sight...but Masterson was a sadist at heart. She deliberately made her new lover wait excruciatingly long periods of time before he felt her crisp black leather glove across his backside. He was trapped in her web of vermillion sex. She reduced him to an object, and he obeyed her every wish. Nothing was taboo; but, she could not bring Drew to tears, as hard as she tried. She would love this one until she accomplished her red task.

EIGHT

During the pre-dawn hours of some Sunday Sinatra morning we jumped the gates of Graceland. Security guards showed their ugly Confederate faces and I immobilized them one by one with a forty-five caliber tranquilizer gun. In silhouette, the guards were felled, one after another; seismic thuds interrupting the morning quiet until every last fucking one of those bastards were cold gone. A pile of bodies, a Confederate battle lost in dreams. It's blackout at the mansion. In a matter of hours we would be able to remove the corpse of the greatest singer in the short history of recorded music.

As I approached the gold grave-site, I gave Calvin the positive sign...a nod...he motioned to come closer.

"This tomb is deactivated...you sick white bastards."

"Are you absolutely sure?"

"There are three hot wire leads. The red is specifically for the perimeter of the estate and the gravesite...you took care of that!" he whispered, his breath pure adrenaline excitement. "Blue wire is for activating the bronze marker, and then the green lead is either wired up to the casket or the King himself. I won't know for sure until we dig the bastard up. We are clear."

I squeezed Calvin by the lapels of his overalls and said, too loudly, "Tell me again...it's a done deal."

"Go get that white asshole...tell him to start digging...we're clear."

This is too wild. "You're making history Mr. Washington...there are hundreds of oriental freaks that are going to pay through the ass...to dust their American Corn Flakes in the Far East morning breakfast of their fetish. **POWDERED ELVIS BONES,** the essence of the King to start your day...this is too big...too fuckin' big."

I raced back to the Mansion and...Stop...What? I found Diamond Dog masturbating in Elvis' master bath.

"Oh man...I've always wanted to do this...jack it in the same toilet where The King took his final seat on the throne...take a picture Billy...take a fuckin' picture...we can sell them to some Presley perverts...start a new fetish line...ya know."

I didn't understand why I had to stand there and deal with that, why this delay was forcing me to witness Diamond Dog's sick fetish, but he went on. Talked his way through the process because this was the only way the sick fuck could finish. He seemed to be focusing on a cockroach climbing along the edge of the toilet bowl, aiming for him, waiting, breathing heavily while...

"They can't get rid of all infestations...Termiticide involves two things, either a poison that forces the insect away from home where they forget where they live and starve, or another poison trick that inhibits the secretion allowing the termite to shed its exoskeleton, no excretion no growth, they crush to death...Different for the cockroach. The poison has to be ingested and taken back to the sick hive where they eat each other's waste and even each other's corpses, a society founded on cannibalism and scat munching...They ingest the death from the poisoned member of the group willingly, the millions of eggs wait in obedience...cockroaches only have those two instincts, a binary thought pattern...Seeking out darkness or seeking out their incestuous social group...This is how the poison kills them all...Attacks the neurotransmitters...causes uterine and pineal gland cancer in lab rats...We only see cockroaches when there's an overpopulation problem at the hive, they get evicted...the poison works so well, so, so well because it's that habitual group mind that gets destroyed by its own desire, its *own desire...*"

That's when the clear shot load hit its intended target, sending the cockroach spinning, landing behind the toilet back to the darkness it was seeking. I couldn't take much more of this. We were also on the brink of being destroyed by our own desires. Snap out of it!

"Get the FUCK outside you SICK LUNATIC!"

"Billy."

"What!"

"Ah...should I flush it?"

"WHAT?"

"You know...should I lose those twelve million screamin'

sperm? Send them down to Davy Jones' locker? Into the briny deep?"

"Leave it...CHRIST...LET'S GO."

"Leave it...come on...oh...I...I get it...sort of like a...ahh."

"YEAH A FUCKING GIFT FOR PRISCILLA, MOVE!"

It took one hour to remove the bronze marker that labeled the grave...another hour to dig down to the concrete bunker that enclosed the coffin...two hours to remove the concrete lid...and another forty minutes to hoist the gold plated casket out of the cold, dark Memphis dirt hole.

Calvin was right...the King was hot-wired...and that's when Calvin started to get weird. He started to rant about HOODOO and VOODOO and WITCH DOCTOR SHIT. How grave robbers were destined to GO TO HELL...and the WHITE FUCKIN' GHOST OF THE KING...WILL SEEK REVENGE ON OUR LOST SOULS.

My patience was gone. "SHUT UP CALVIN AND GET A GRIP! THE FAT BASTARD'S PROBABLY NOT EVEN IN HERE!"

Diamond Dog stood wide-eyed peering down at the casket. Calvin took several steps back. And I proceeded to slowly lift the lid of the King's Tomb.

At first it creaked like the sound of a rusty hinge being jimmied off a junked, forgotten door. I lifted the lid about two inches when the Dog whispered "...what's that smell...can't you smell that?"

Then Calvin…"Yeah, the Dog's right. I can smell it TOO…DEAR GOD IN HEAVEN!"

"IT'S BACON CHEEZ WHIZ…ASSHOLE…THAT'S WHAT IT IS…Vernon must have put a six-pack of FUCKIN' CHEEZ WHIZ into the casket before they buried him…what a sick bunch of Egyptian tomb pharaoh get-ready-for-the-next world bullshit! RELAX…we must have punctured one of the cans…RELAX."

"Oh…shit…that ain't no cocksucking cheese smell…that's…THAT'S THE VAPOR OF SORCERY…COME…COME TO STRANGLE US ALL…THE PHARAOH'S CURSE! DEAR JESUS FORGIVE MEEEEEEE!"

"SHUT THE FUCK UP CALVIN!"

"NO MAN…NO…IT'S A WARNING…DON'T LIFT THAT LID…DEAR GOD IN HEAVEN PLEASE…DON'T."

And with that last BESEECH ringing in my ears I threw open the lid…and there he was…THE KING OF ROCK AND ROLL. Here was the MOTHER LODE. Exactly as I'd expected, Elvis was laid out in a white rhinestone studded Colonel Parker jump suit. The skin of the corpse was decomposed…it resembled spent latex, distorted, his features somewhat forgotten. The hair and the sideburns were miraculously intact, still hanging on to the skull like residual memories of the Kingdom.

Ten rings...diamonds...rubies...emeralds...adorned his skeletal fingers. The fingernails had fallen off. I scooped them up and placed them in my shirt pocket. We would smoke them later. The King wore matching Rolex watches on both wrists...and when I threw off the cold coverlet to expose the entire corpse...his feet were clad in...yes...blue suede shoes. MOTHER LODE INDEED.

And then it HAPPENED.

To this day...I still can't believe it happened. See...Calvin decided to wait back at the truck...this was understandable. He was worried shitless about African curses...and witches...and mojo...and charms and specters. And before I could load the King into a black vinyl body bag...The Dog had also disappeared.

I started to remove the rings...and then I heard the unmistakable twang and shudder of a swimming pool diving board reverberate through the night sky. The Dog, that psycho bastard, decided to fuckin' CANNONBALL into the family pool...and when that diving board oscillated vertically toward its highest apex, it set off the only remaining security link inside of Graceland.

Before the Dog even hit the warm, chlorinated water, the mansion was engulfed in an unbelievable array of flood-lights that swept across the grounds. The sirens that were set off pierced my ears bloody. Within seconds, two Tennessee State Police helicopters hovered overhead shining triangular shafts of white light down upon the Mansion. Squad cars began to screech and halt...and along the perimeter...the horrendous sound of bullhorns punctured the aerial light show.

MOTHER...FUCK!

I grabbed the King's head by the jaw and inserted both of my thumbs into the eye sockets, twisting and wrenching his skull until it came apart at just above his clavicle. Amazingly the splenius...sternohyoid and sternocleidomastoid held the skull in place. They must have embalmed the bastard with SUPER GLUE. I bent and convoluted the skull upward and out of the casket until it finally snapped clean with a CRACK at about the fourth vertebrae. I tossed the King's skull into the body bag and ran toward the back of the mansion...what a fucking rush...these bastards are going to start shooting...that was the last thing I wanted...a shootout with Tennessee Troopers...and they would shoot to kill...since I just fucked over the tomb of the Pharaoh of Memphis. As mad wild as this was...I could not stop thinking about the remains that were left: scapula...humerus...ulna...radius...clavicle...THE WHOLE DAMN SKELETON...femur...patella...tibia...fibula...ALL IN PAIRS...I was going to be sick. What the hell am I going to collect...just for the head? Guess I'll have to sell the nails, no smoke down post celebration. And then the reality of the moment set in hard and fast...Houdini could not get out of this TRAP!

I flew past the rear of the Mansion and headed for the huge garage where the cars are stored...I needed to catch my breath...gather my senses. I can feel a dark doom closing in on this early two hours past midnight Monday morning pillage. Within seconds the Dog came splashing from the opposite direction...I could have shot the psycho bastard.

"HOLY FUCK BILLY HOLY FUCK."

"RELAX KID...RELAX."

"THE PLACE IS CRAWLING WITH FUCKIN' BADGES...WE COULD GET THE FUCKIN' CHAIR BILLY...THE FUCKIN' CHAIR!"

"RELAX DOG...LET ME THINK."

"THINK? FUCKIN' THINK? GET US OUT OF HERE BILLY...GET US OUT OF HERE...NOW!"

"PAY ATTENTION KID...WE'RE GOING TO MAKE A RUN FOR THE TRUCK...THROUGH THOSE HEDGES...OVER THE FENCE...TO THE BOULEVARD."

"WHAT? YOU THINK THAT WILLIE MAYS MOTHERFUCKIN' HO IS STILL WAITING FOR US...CHRIST...THEY HAVE THAT BLACK BASTARD STRUNG UP...HE'S SPILLING HIS GUTS RIGHT NOW, BILLY!"

"HE AIN'T NO FUCKIN' PUNK...RELAX."

Then...the ground shook. What sounded like a detonation...a massive explosion...WHAM! That crazy-mad superstitious Calvin crashed the truck through the galvanized fence that surrounds the rear perimeter of the estate. He was followed by two screaming squad cars with emergency lights flashing and echoing off the buildings. Sparks engulfing Bodies by Fischer. He took out a row of dense hedges and an old wooden tool shed...tools sent flying like war zone shrapnel...and screeched to a halt.

"GET IN...NOW!'

I jumped in the front seat and the Dog flew into the back of the truck bed...we were airborne in milliseconds and the Dog bounced around in the bed of the truck like a loose goof golf ball. Red...white...and blue lights crisscrossed overhead as we ripped ass down a steep incline chewing up yards of green grass. The helicopters had us locked in sight with their floodlights...and the interior of the truck cab was lit up like a pinball machine. Calvin smashed the gas pedal to the floor...down shifted into second and caromed off of two peach trees before crashing through the gates of Graceland ...DAMN!...onto Presley Boulevard.

The night air was criminally bloated with the redolence of scorched foliage...burnt metal...smoked rubber...and defiled soil. Roasted photons. This was serious. Dangerous. I could taste the adrenalin on my tongue as we raced into a tunnel to get the helicopters off our ass. Then Calvin mashed on the brakes and we slammed to a stop.

Waiting in the Harding Tunnel was a 1970 convertible El Dorado with one driver, armed.

"GET OUT...GET OUT NOW."

"COME ON KID...LET'S GO."

Silence. The Diamond Dog was gone. SHIT! Me and Calvin hopped into the Cadillac and I stuffed the skull under the back seat. Fueled by an unmatched level of tripped out intensity, we went truly berserker and drove out of that tunnel like we owned it...and we DID!

Post Escape Debrief

Memphis. The escape.

"Man, Billy! What the fuck are we going to do if the heat comes down?"

"Relax kid, nothing to worry about. Maybe your God's looking after the mansion," I smiled. I stared at his young Christian blue eyes and shook my head in comic disgust. Another poor bastard fed to the deep yellow hole of belief. I lit a cigarette. The kid played with his cold, runny breakfast eggs. I politely motioned to the waitress, making the coffee distress signal. The kid forked a greasy sausage, and before he could place it in his mouth, I slapped the sausage against the restaurant window.

"Don't eat that shit. Pigs are killers. A filthy fat beast."

He looked at the greasy splash on the window and the blurry landscape beyond. Cocking his head he lowered his sight down in the direction of the lost meat. While he was reaching for it with his fork I squashed it under the left heel of my boot.

"Sausage and egg are my life force," he mumbled while looking down at the wreckage of his breakfast.

"Order some pancakes, shut the fuck up, I'm saving your life."

"I don't understand why we don't just leave town."

"I was at a party. Listen to me. Back in college, everyone was laid out in the living room watching Gone With The Wind not because we wanted to but because we were too stoned to change the channel. Quiet, I want to say it was 1:00 am, nothing but suburban silence and streetlights shining down on vacant streets. This was a humid midsummer night. Frank was upstairs hopped up on something that sent him in a completely different direction than the rest of us, so he couldn't hang. DAPDAPDAPDAPDAPDAP! It happened that fast. Frank ran down the stairs firing a semi-automatic into the ceiling and ran straight out the front door into the street, continuing the explosion of bullets into the air and destroying the peace completely."

"What did you do when the cops showed up?"

"That's just it. They didn't. Sometimes a crime is so horrible that when you're confronted with the reality... I just imagine the sleepy, startled faces of the suburbanites jolted out of their beds. No

58

doubt they pulled the sheets over their heads, turned over and tried to forget it forever. *Forever. That's how people deal with the Big Strange. Graceland? Who knows what kind of surreal things have gone down inside those walls? All kings must die young to preserve what was originally unique during their rule. The crazy fallout will be forgotten. Add to that the fact that there's no God. This God that you reference in conversation is a televised God. He got cancelled. The rest is just inferior syndication."*

"It's an infomercial," the kid said, and then spooned up and swallowed his cold snot eggs.

Jewell looked at me with a smirk of painted disdain. "You don't expect me to swallow all of that...horseshit?"

"It's not shit...it's true...all of it...let's forget it."

"You expect me..." she closed her eyes with a boredom bordering on annoyance. "Wait, wait...you expect me to believe that you and some kid psychopath along with a black felon...robbed the grave of Elvis Presley. THE Elvis Presley?"

"That's..."

"No, wait, let me finish...and after you had the corpse in your hands...the sociopath decided to go for a swim...in Graceland?"

"Yes...and."

"And then you lost the young freak and you and fuckin' Uncle Ben...make your getaway in a convertible Cadillac...with the skull stashed under the seat?"

"Hey…forget it…let's go, you drive."

"No, no, no, no…So tell me why didn't this story make CNN or Hard Copy or Dan Rather…HUH?"

"Because the authorities decided to cover it up…this is America."

"The AUTHORITIES, of course!" She laughed. "Ok, I'll go along with it, why?"

"MONEY…the Presley Estate is valued at…what? Six hundred million, or something approaching that figure. It behooved everyone involved to keep the lid on…because if the public ever found out that Elvis' skull was stolen from the crypt…it would have financially and spiritually devalued the estate. The entire Presley myth and tourist attraction. GONE. That kind of information is damaging, and that damage is irreparable and must be suppressed at all costs. YOUR CHRIST! Just think about all those freaks who gather in Memphis from points across the globe, a real fucking pilgrimage to a sacred site, America's civil religion, one of our only true saints. What would happen to all those supplicants if they ever found out that they were praying to the headless priest of ROCK AND ROLL?"

"This is NONSENSE."

"Let's go."

"So tell me Billy…where's the head? Where are the fingernails? Where's Calvin? Where's the fuckin' jewelry, huh?"

"Please…let's go back to the apartment…please."

"NO. Not until you finish this bullshit story. We've burned up enough time on this, so finish!"

"How many beers are left?"

"Six."

"Alright. Sit back and relax, it'll get weird."

"Weird, huh."

I gave her a stern look. She bit her lower lip…and reclined in the cold sand of Revere. I opened two beers…took a slug of Grand Marnier…the night blue black sky hummed with jet airliners on their way to Logan…the beach was deserted…cold autumn waves of the North Atlantic became silent.

"I only had time to remove one of the rings and one Rolex. I ended up giving them to Calvin as a bonus. What he eventually did with them I'm not sure, because I never saw him again. Now the fingernails are a whole 'nother cup of fish. Down in the Gulf of Mexico I sold five of the fingernails in Pascagoula, Mississippi…to the High Priest of a Latin American Satanic Cult."

"I can't take any more of this."

"SHUT UP. I was introduced to this ecclesiastic monster by a couple I had met at the Flor-Bama Club. Thomas worked as an orderly at the Pensacola Sanitarium for the Criminally Insane and his squeeze was a Hells Angel biker slut with some serious problems of her own. We drank, talked, and I mentioned the contraband. The next day I was introduced to Emanuel Lorga...Lord of the Dead."

"Dear God."

"Lorga was a known Satan worshipper... some kind of Venezuelan vampire. He drank whole blood for breakfast, shit like that. Scary fuck. So Lorga somehow became privy to the semi-failed heist even before I was introduced to him. And I told him the same story I just told you. I offered to sell him the whole set of fingernails for eight thousand dollars."

"So...over a case of Budweiser...I cut a deal with the Mad Mephistopheles. He believed the plunder was authentic...you can't fool one of these plasma priests. So I sold him five of the fingernails for four thousand. Gave Thomas and Vicky a ten percent finder's fee...four hundred dollars...and planned on smoking the remainder of the right handed nails. See...Lorga wanted only the nails from the left hand...he said that the White Prince of Eternity...your GOD...created the Universe with his right hand and that the left hand was the infinite limb of SIN, The Magic Hand, symbolic of Satan himself."

Jewell did not believe a word. She made the gesture, a spinning finger next to the side of the head that meant CRAZY when I mentioned smoking the King's polished fingernails. I decided it would behoove me not to show her the skull which was chilling in the trunk of the New Yorker. During the drive back to the apartment she slept, curled up in the front seat, her windswept black hair brushing my right thigh. I believe I was legally drunk, and then the Freudian double kicks in. This was more than just an illusion of an illusion. This psycho-trance was substantive; it is physical and hyper-real.

Barbie Doll, that bitch should die. That billion dollar sex gender propaganda machine that chews the holy assholes out of adolescent girls brainwashed straight to the alter of their choice which was already chosen for them. Alright, if we have to be bombarded with the plastic white whore, then let me purchase the Barbie with the colostomy hole...the synthetic eight inch sculpture surgically repaired with the high school incision. The stinking medical dent orifice, the soul opening where the Christmas cookies ooze stench and waste. Yes, don't my Barbie look fine with that plastic bag hanging off her white plastic hip, or the crack addicted Barbie, whoring her way across Suffolk Downs to suck on Bolivian terrorists. A black eye damaged sex catastrophe, the dejected blue vulgar lung of cocaine commodity or the amputated figurine, yes; the pink polymerized debutante lost both legs changing her tire on that cute pink sports car, lost her balance on her ballerina pointed feet and got sideswiped by a drunken Floridian hauling eighteen wheels of steel. Lost her legs right at the knees, now that's the Barbie Doll, the crippled virgin advertising the cold cardboard sign that says "Will Ass Fuck For Food."

No, give me the doll with scurvy, the only one for your lost lesbian daughter, screw that, give me Barbie Cancer, Barbie in the

oncology ward, the white, withering nymph of a new holocaust that
turns into the fall down anorexic Barbie of Hollywood.

Barbie, the new hallucination will be Serial Killer Uterine
Barbie...Ted Bundy's recessive gene niece, the saint with the
straight razor carving her way across blue televised America. Slice
the nuts off a young quarterback from Indiana. Carve the Catholic
brain out of an old yellow Nun. Cook the grey matter in a new
Costco microwave. Dahmer Barbie. Whew, she's got body parts in
the refrigerator of her dream house. Everyone knows Barbie needs
new clothes.

"What do you call all of this?"

"Bend over Barbie."

I carried the sleeping Jewell up three flights of stairs and
she invited me to spend the evening with her. We drank black
coffee and smoked.

On the first of November I made an appointment with Dr.
Elizabeth St. James, 1675 Providence Street, Boston, MA. I
noticed her advertisement in Boston Magazine. She's a
psychiatrist, her picture featured prominently in the ad, which I
thought was unusual.

Drop dead gorgeous, and that's the only reason I made the
appointment. The meeting was set for Monday at 3pm, making me
her last specimen of scrutiny for her day, and mine for that matter.

Dr. St. James was a stunning natural redhead who stood six
feet tall when wearing her green suede Kenneth Cole pumps.

She was a beautiful combination of fragrance, manicured nails, soft skin and carefully applied makeup. On occasions when she crossed and uncrossed her stockinged legs, I swear I sensed her robust ovulation through the heated synthetic nylon. Her breasts were well proportioned as was her hard, ample rump. This would be a great day of mutual scrutiny, a tennis match of perceptions.

Her office was decked out with all the obligatory diplomas hanging in an aesthetically pleasing manner, the remnants of time spent between pages and words. Her throne of dark burgundy was crowned with a Warhol Campbell's soup can print circa 1965. The carpeting was a pale industrial grey and the chair in which I sat was designed with the Bauhaus in mind. She introduced herself.

I stared at the beautiful doctor and was overcome with vicious candy thoughts of conquest. A glistening pair of silver surgical scissors stood at attention in a hand painted vase... and...I wanted to grab those shears and cut a three inch hole into her immaculate hose right at the crotch, forcing her now splayed legs open wider still and roughly bite the red hair that protected her pink nub. She would attempt to engage the silent security alarm but I would pin her arms under her startled ass and have my sadistic way with this lovely professional. Wisps of frayed nylon would become lodged in my teeth like a pervert's dental floss. I would bite and lick her slit until she passed out from multi-orgasmic oxygen deprivation. "Is it alright if I call you Billy?" she said, breaking the spell of my fantasy.

I thought is it alright if I call you a pair of big rose colored nipples who can't get enough white cock down her Cambridge throat? "Ah, yes, Billy is fine, doctor," I relented.

"Great, now let's get started. From reviewing your recently signed medical form, I see you circled 'Manic Depressive'. Have you read about manic depression? Does manic depression run in your family?"

"No."

"I see, then why do you think you're manic depressive?"

"Mood swings."

"What kind of mood swings?"

I started to laugh, I couldn't help it. The shit that was unloading out of my head and her questions, I couldn't stop. "I'm sorry."

"These mood swings, do they come and go very frequently, or do their durations last for longer periods of time?"

"No."

She said nothing, just stared into my eyes. Glancing down, she wrote something very fast on a legal pad with green ink. Green ink, the color of money.

"Can you tell me about your personal history, about your parents, anything?"

"My father Frank was a brain damaged alcoholic Vietnam war vet. My mother, Brett Ford, is a frigid junior high science teacher."

"Why do you describe your mother as frigid?"

"Well, ah, Frank used to always complain about not getting laid. He used to call me the Immaculate Conception. Brett finally left Frank when I graduated from high school. At times it was a violent mess, but hey, water off a duck's ass."

"Now please don't be put off by my questioning, but I need to ask you some questions about your sexual behavior. Alright?"

I sat on the edge of the chair and leaned forward in her direction to see if I could make her uncomfortable. I was trying to violate that imaginary bubble that educated psycho-heads like to pontificate about. Did she learn about sexual behavior from her psych books first, or by experience? Which of the two fed her need to go into this field of work? "Sure," I said.

"Do you masturbate?"

"What?"

"Let me explain. Research shows that manic depressives are habitual masturbators, not all, mind you, but most. It's just a starting point. I hope I haven't made you feel uncomfortable."

Why the hell did I have to circle manic depression? I should have checked delusional schizophrenic with homosexual tendencies. I needed more entertainment from this, let's have some fun. "Yes, sometimes I'll choke the rooster and then drink a box of import, get shit faced before Letterman comes on."

She smiled. She was obviously pleased with herself, like she cracked the ice. The small mouth noises coming out of her painted lips were called words, rephrased from other words she'd read in those textbooks, markings on paper, reconfirmed by an authoritative source, a professor, and reworked toward a thesis, approved by a committee who'd read similar markings on paper and language, all this language. All this language failed to capture the habits of human animals. Nothing about the chemical fate of DNA that combines with circumstance, bloodstream, incoming sensations and a touch of magic that determines what's next for this carbon based life form, never the same decisions, changing moment to moment. Everything we do based on delusions and inspiration, the ridiculous and the sublime linked together through every moment. None of this is what we are, and that's why I was so amused. I wondered what her thesis subject was about, some abnormal psychology based on an old college boyfriend with a weird kink? The words on paper put it all nicely in a box for her. I wasn't about to get in the box.

"I see," she whispered. "A habitual masturbator with a drinking problem."

Here we go. "I don't have a drinking problem."

"Sorry, that was terribly presumptuous. How much alcohol do you consume on a daily basis?"

"Around a case a day."

"I see, now tell me when did you become fixated on your penis?"

Ok sister, you want to go deep? You want to go for the long ball, the high fast one? "It all started when I was in the seventh grade, riding the Woodlawn Bus from Franklin Avenue to Maratta Road. There was something with the juxtaposition of diesel fuel and mass transportation vibrations that made me want to relieve myself in my lunch box before physical education."

"Yes, can you continue?"

"I guess I became fixated on my cock when it decided to grow on its own. I would be in church and the bastard decided to grow, there was nothing I could do about it. In fact I tried clubbing it to death on several occasions, but it just persisted in its engorged, bloated indifference to my own horror. Once I wacked it with a ball peen hammer right on the pink hole head, I was at the local cinema, I believe it was a Dracula flick. Nothing. I could not kill that unholy beast."

She continued to write and talk simultaneously. "I see, what you were experiencing was puberty, there was no need to become involved with self-flagellation."

She was trying to provoke me into some ugly scene. Relax. I sat back in the chair, silent. I crossed my right leg over my left and stared again at the lovely doctor.

"You can ask any question you want, professor, but I have concerns, concerns about confidentiality, do you understand?"

"I'm not quite sure I..."

"You understand perfectly," I could feel a gasket starting to blow – hers. "I have a genuine concern for privacy and I would hate to see these sessions become public knowledge, made available to the authorities, and if that is your intent we should discontinue this session immediately."

"Billy, whatever is said in this office stays in this office, period!"

"And what if the records are subpoenaed by the State's Attorney General, are you going to go to jail in the name of psychiatric confidentiality, are you going to prison for me?"

"I must obey the law."

"FUCK the law!"

"Let's cross that bridge when we..."

"Please, no clichés, they're unbecoming."

"Billy there's no need for this conversation. My professional conduct has never been questioned or compromised."

"You're a phony, I'm out of here."

"Please, sit back down. I can help you."

"Later!

"Wait, what could you possibly be reluctant to tell me that you think would lead to a criminal investigation?"

"I can't answer that."

"Tell me."

"I know where Oswald is."

"Excuse me?"

"Lee Harvey, I know where he is."

"The man who shot President Kennedy? Billy, Oswald is dead. Jack Ruby shot him on live television."

"That's what they want you to believe, Elizabeth! Sure everyone saw that fat fuck Ruby shoot Oswald, but did you see Oswald DIE?"

"Oswald is dead, let's focus on you."

I had her going, she didn't know what time it was. I imagined that Elizabeth was thinking she had a full-blown nutcase on her hands. I envisioned her writing a massive thesis that would be published by the New England Journal of Medicine. New combinations of words spoken and written, a different Morse code tapping out the secret coordinates to some new uncharted location of crazy. How they'd congratulate her when she summarized that she'd ultimately CURED a forty year old homicidal male schizophrenic with an assortment of anti-depressants and electroshock therapy. She'd rapidly rise to the top of her profession and later be appointed by the First

Lady to the post of Queen Czarina of mental disorders. She would write the bestseller...cable...then retire to Vermont where she would raise llamas on a diet of lithium and plain yogurt.

"Billy, let's stop this. Oswald is dead."

"Look, I saw Oswald in Cuba in 1986. I was a cub reporter for the Gulf Shore Examiner. Castro had him imprisoned in a hacienda close to Hemingway's Estate. When I saw Lee, he was bouncing a fourteen year old caramel colored Cuban girl on his knee and ingesting large quantities of painkillers. Although he was a prisoner of the Cuban dictator, he was and he wasn't. See, Castro cut a deal with Johnson and the Dallas Police Department to fly the wounded Oswald out of Dallas to the island in exchange for Fidel's promise not to attempt any more assassinations."

"Mr. Ball, please. I think we should end this session."

"Hell, if you did your homework you'd find out that on the fifth of November of the following year the remaining Kennedy brother, Teddy, was secretly flown to Cuba by the CIA and he interviewed a stoned Lee Harvey in person. He spilled his guts to the Catholic bastard, told them the whole fucked conspiracy. By the time Teddy arrived back in Washington, President Johnson clamped the lid shut on the Warren investigation and set into action his plans for the extermination of the North Vietnamese. Welcome to the NEW GENOCIDE, Texas Style!"

Dr. St. James looked at me with bored disbelief. She'd mentally checked out a while ago. It was a sustained look of incredulity. Her painted whore red lips were now parted and unbecoming. Her lawn green eyes appeared dilated with disgust. I sat patiently and waited for another question.

"Billy, let's....leave all this out and talk about the word TRUTH."

"The truth. Sure. Go ahead."

"Great, now do you know the meaning of the word truth?"

"Yes."

"Do you believe in the truth?"

"Perhaps."

"What I'm trying to ascertain is whether you know the difference between the truth and a lie."

"Absolutely."

"What you recently described, well, do you feel it is the truth?"

"Absolutely."

"Do you ever lie?'

"Absolutely."

"Are you lying now?"

"No."

"I see. Can you give me a situation when it would be appropriate to lie?"

"Like a situation when it would be acceptable."

"No, I mean a situation when it would be unacceptable."

"There are no such situations," I proclaimed. This was it; she was going to finally diagnose me with some strange new strain of mental illness. I could feel those wheels turning in her mind.

"Can you give me an example of when it is acceptable to tell an unacceptable lie?"

Elizabeth felt clever asking this question, I could tell. A sly, educated gash with an adroit ability at semantic gymnastics. I paused, and with a pensive look on my face, I ran my left middle finger across my left eyebrow and said, "...when you're in a court of law."

She blinked. "You find it acceptable and appropriate to blatantly lie under oath in a court of law?"

"Absolutely."

"Please expound."

I looked that beautiful Cambridge dish dead in the green eye and laid it on her "Because I don't believe in your God or the laws of this nation. What man or woman – who gave them the right to adorn a robe and declare themselves judge over me? What magistrate, executive judge, justice of the peace or chief justice can force me to obey their laws when they coerce your God into the equation? I thought there was a separation between church and state, at least in theory. Your Christ! IN GOD WE TRUST is on the money. Let's get down to the legal version of the truth versus a lie, especially if the imaginary guy is listening? No respect for that system, a system with the scales of justice weighted down with corruption. A system of justice polluted by false men and defiled laws. Shall I continue?"

"Yes, please."

"I won't be caged in by man or your God. Yes I think it's always appropriate and acceptable to lie if the marble walls of society are smeared with shame and dishonor. Nothing can really stop a widespread lie from becoming the truth, that's the only acceptable definition. Truth as a widespread lie we've decided to believe in, in a country where disinformation is sold by the pound? Yes. Lie."

"Do you believe in the American Flag?"

"FUCK your flag. The war author, James Jones, flew to Washington before he passed away. He viewed all the monuments on the Mall, all of the glorious and heavenly erectiles. The Lincoln, the Jefferson, the Vietnam Memorial. And when he was done viewing all of this magnum opus to America, when his dying eyes could not register a single light wave more of patriotic column, pillar, gravestone or shrine, he CRIED. He said it was all beautiful bullshit. In school they called it 'civil religion.' No country, flag and affiliated court of law would even recognize the truth coming from anyone's lips. Can you understand THAT?"

Dr. Elizabeth St. James registered bored disgust and more than a tinge of nervousness. Her frequencies were jammed, had no reference for these mouth noises and stopped processing it all. Stop. She collected herself, wrote some fast notes with that green money ink anyway, because that's what she does, and asked if I could attend another session.

"No, Twilight's Last Gleaming!" She said nothing as I headed for the door and made my way to the Combat Zone.

"This is what I'm talking about, Billy." Masterson *deadpanned in that future moment when the restaurant bar felt more like a courtroom where I'm always on trial.* "You're a fucking hate-fueled dictatorial hothead." *I continued to order our meal, ignoring her cruel mood for now.* "All your conspiracy theories about everything and nothing, it just gets boring. And your hatred for every cultural and social group..."

The peace we had while eating didn't last long. She was out for blood. "Call the chef over to the fucking table; you know you never could pick a decent restaurant to save your ass." *She was slurring and had officially entered the region known as Too Much Wine.*

The chef approached the table, already wearing an expression of wide-eyed conciliatory concern, "Is there something wrong, Miss?" *Masterson sipped her wine, sneering and steeling herself for what's next.* "You expect me to eat this rack of mutton?"

"Miss, I'll get you another if you're displeased."

"You got some balls on you, white boy, serving this old meat as lamb." She picked up her plate and before the chef could take hold of it she dropped it on the floor, shattering the plate and scattering the food, hunks of meat and bone.

"But ma'am, I prepared it myself. The lamb didn't even have teeth."

I had to shut her down. "Stop it with your fucking mouth and settle down, just settle down." "Settle down. SETTLE DOWN?" She'd turned on me now, the chef escaped. "Remember that time we rented a house in Montauk during that 4th of July weekend? Don't say a fucking word to me you creep! All these years you had me brainwashed. You took my virginity at sixteen, sixteen you bastard!"

Everyone else in the restaurant bar sat in rapt silence, taking it all in. Shit, that's what I would've done if this whole dagger story wasn't pressed on my jugular. "In Montauk, I got my period, remember? Remember?" She was looking inquisitively at not just me but the whole restaurant audience as if they had the cosmic ability to confirm her cycle. Please God, make this stop.

"You left the house for two hours saying you were going to buy a thousand dollar an hour hooker named Cherry you'd heard about, and that if I wanted to come along I could watch!" The audience was laughing now, she was losing sympathy and it didn't help her state of mind. "You damaged me, Billy! Fuck you, and fuck your mother. If I ever see that bitch I'll kick her in the cunt for giving

77

birth to you! I'm joining a convent anyway. I'm a nun, or I'm going to be. Stay the fuck away from me. Don't send me any more gifts or boxes or airplane tickets or books or records, I'm done."

The waitress placed a new rack of lamb in front of her just in time to see Masterson shaking, grabbing her purse and staggering away from the table.

"Fuck you and your Jesus!" I shouted to her as she went out the door. The audience applauded.

She's milk
Expired
May eighth
Drink up

NINE

A Fleetwood Mac TUSK bass drum thudding in my head woke me from the black, dreamless sleep that only one six-pack turning into three could produce. I ate an unorthodox breakfast of fried lamb chop...blade cut...and green onions. Four cups of black, no sugar, silenced the marching band. At ten o'clock I started to feel ill. There was a knock at the door...it was Jewell. She held a pipe with hash and two quarts of chilled Beaujolais as an offering... She sat down at the kitchen table in her white cotton bath robe. I wondered what was underneath while I washed two wine glasses in the kitchen sink overfilled with dirty dishes...poured wine for two...smoked her Iranian sedative. The bare overhead light bulb strobed thirteen irregular flashes in one final Morse code SOS before it blew out. Nothing for me to do but light six blessed yellow candles all adorned with crucifixes...in primary color scheme...she sat across from me in the low light...crossed her legs...exposed holy white thighs...she spoke, a stoned black-haired vision with dark eyes flattened by wine. She started to cry. Wiping her tears on the collar of her robe, she poured another glass...motioning my way with the bottle...I declined. She said that today was the third anniversary of her younger brother's death...shot dead through the throat...a drive by shooting at a Detroit Lions game. It was the calendar date memory causing her to slowly pull her fingers through her long hair in frustrated disgust, refreshed bereavement on a desolate morning. We smoked again. Her unpainted lips quivered...a tear spilled onto her breast...her hand wiped it upwards toward her thin silver necklace.

"Why Billy...why?"

"Because the spectacle disempowers the spectator."

"What?"

"It's hidden...people don't like to admit it...but it is real." She refilled the wine glasses and asked me to continue...I thought it was the wrong moment but she insisted, so I lit a Marlboro, exhaled. "It's a universal phenomenon...a tragic hidden aspect of society. There was a malignant masquerade of power hungry sports owners...worldwide...that create these unfortunate events...A VIRUS...all in the name of a Universal Capitalism." I didn't want to convert her authentic grief into another useless currency, but she insisted.

"Look...your brother was not murdered because of some drunken unfortunate fanaticism at the Silver Dome. This has nothing to do with the competition...or too much alcohol...or because of fate. That's the disinformation that is presented via satellite technology through mass sporting advertising...the transmitter of communication. Your brother became one with the universe because the exhibition smashed the beholder. THE SPECTACLE DISMPOWERED THE SPECTATOR."

"I get where you're coming from, but I don't want SOCIOLOGY...I want REVENGE." She wanted stainless retaliation...swift, leaving no trace...she wanted to cut the nuts off those bastards that wiped her sibling off the face of the earth...she wanted pure manic vampire BLOOD retaliation. VIOLENCE.

"WOULDYOUKILLTHEMFORME," she shouted, the wine dulling her sentence into a slur of almost unintelligible vowels...but I heard. Loud and clear.

"I hardly know you." I laughed.

"I'll pay you," she smiled. "If you...say...had known me for a year...and if we were lovers...would you kill them then?"

I tried to pour more wine but the visual field shifted, swayed...spilling some on the white table cloth...no attempt was made to rescue the coverlet from the bright burgundy stain...the room and its contents already too far gone. Damn, it was too early in the morning for such mad punk philosophical discourse but now...too high...lit another cigarette.

"Yes...I would make an attempt to murder the creeps if the opportunity presented itself." She seemed relieved...her eyes now shifting fragments on one side of a Picasso face...refracted stoned bursts of candlelight. "If you are going to seek personal retribution then you be smart about it. Leave no witnesses...no evidence. You just can't fly off the handle and murder some adversary in a fuckin' McDonald's...with twenty ten observers."

She cackled quietly to herself at his high math and then…"The trick is to murder or maim but not get caught…and after the deed is done…you certainly cannot feel guilty about it. This is imperative…Life with a guilty conscience leaves a trail wherever you've been and when they see you coming, they'll know where you've been." We both laughed at this stoned affirmation.

She smiled. "You're serious about this?"

"Absolutely. Fuck those bastards that heap guilt and sin onto your psyche. Free yourself from this psychological yoke. They want you to feel horrible about everything that does not conform to their agenda, break you down and shove those pieces up your beautiful ass." She blushed. "To hell with their commandments, values, morals. This is control. Any time you doubt yourself you're ready to be a consumer and a slave. Fits with the agenda."

I poured more wine and we shared the pipe, again. There was a sweet angelic aura glowing around her face, an angel with a big gun. "And never ever turn yourself in, never rat out your own hole. This is so fucking stupid, America. Earth. A failed experiment, virus run amok in the form of the human race. No one wants Veronica Jewell thinking like this. They brainwash us as soon as we escape from the fuck hole." She laughed and covered her mouth. "Schools, churches, family units, jobs, money and POW we're perfectly controlled to lead a choreographed existence based on someone else's plan. Is there life before death? Fuck it all and fuck them, yes, I would kill in the name of your dead brother."

A glassy stoned smile on her face let me know she understood. "So what you're saying is that murder, mayhem, revolution and nonconformity is the answer?"

"No, YOU just said that!"

The following morning I rolled the Chrysler toward New Orleans to meet with Toshiba Ushida. Never saw my cousin, and never saw Jewell again.

Besides, her brother's killers may have wanted to die. I wasn't in the job of granting wishes.

He grabbed at fever.

Any disease he could lay his hands on.

Prayed to God for cancer.

Petitioned the Ghost for congestive heart failure.

Appealed to the Virgin for kidney failure.

Solicited Jesus Christ for multiple sclerosis.

Requested a priest to be afflicted with blinding diabetes.

Begged an old nun to be infected with herpes simplex encephalitis.

Literally drank pints of infected blood.

Engaged in anal sex with HIV infected crack whores.

Swallowed an array of illegal drugs.

Chain smoked five packs of menthol cigarettes a day.

Ate red meat for breakfast.

Drank whiskey from morning until night.

Stared at the sun in bemused contempt.

And in the winter drove a topless white convertible.

Sporting only a t-shirt, slacks and sandals.

Sucked face with an array of influenza infected females.

Injected heroin into his circulatory system.

Dined on mercury infected shellfish.

And salmonella tainted poultry.

Inhaled marijuana hashish and opium for dessert.

Sniffed glue and industrial epoxy.

Ingested flakes of lead paint like candy.

And on Christmas Eve.

In front of the Latham Hotel in Philadelphia.

He was crushed under the wheels of a Port Authority Bus.

And later cursed the attending trauma physicians.

For saving his life.

TEN

During the fourth hour of the haul, somewhere in the state of New York. *All elegance has disappeared with the last stroke of the Maestro...Singer Sargent. Shocking unbearable coffee dog teeth jet through the free ceiling as the last archangel looped through black holes of defeated faith.*

That thin, smooth plastic card became a new crucifix. The holiday cross of the new money changers. As two thousand years of fable and myth and special Pope effects vanish straight up the goat's hole, the black mass of spilled blood. Best Buy, Nixon killed Hoffa, eighty-nine cents a pound.

I saw Buddha the other day. That renunciate was sitting in my backyard. The leaves were turning to their annual death. He's quite a big bastard, all that thinking on the mountaintop has done nothing for his hunting and gathering human machine, a body meant for motion instead of stillness. Silence, we're not built for it. His face is solid silver. He resembled a saintlike gorilla, not the dove. He was pure essence with a fat silver head.

I walked through the broken peeled paint arbor past leaves and weeds, the fecundity of the soft, brown dirt hitting my nostrils. I took a seat opposite Buddha. I had two cheap beers in my hand, unopened. I offered him one and to my surprise, he accepted. Said nothing, of course. He popped the aluminum top and sucked that can clean in record time. Cocksucker is trying to intimidate me. I pulled a small bronze proto pipe out of my pocket and lit the shit, the green tea of Cassady. I offered, he again accepted. They have to take what they're offered. The real Gautama Siddhartha choked on free pork that landed in his begging bowl. How did he handle that date with the now? The translucent ghost of Freudian Vienna blew across the backdrop of my subconscious.

"So what you want, stoned fat boy?" I can't believe I said that, or did I just think it? Fucking Cassady was too strong.

He spoke. "I've come to offer the key, the key to the universal lock. The answer."

I looked the stoned bastard in his silver eyes and took a sip of Detroit's finest monkey piss beer. I spit a hocker aftertaste between my Bally loafers and smiled. Lips together, no teeth showed. He sat, obese and holy, waiting for a response. Fuck him and his sutras and his meditation. I spat again.

"Your HOUSE is DARK, and your COCK is COLD."

What is this stoned shit? I said "WHAT, MUTHAFUCKA?"

Memo to myself: Never, ever call a Buddha a motherfucker.

The stone bastard exploded. A million shards of Buddha Formica rained down upon the point seven acres. Stabs of glass covered every inch of the property extending toward the neighboring houses. The police were of no help. Bloody dogs fell from the heavens. White rabid one winged bats flew against the destruction

heaving rabid foam out of triangular white teeth. The landscape
turned BLOOD INK. I laughed.

It took twenty three hours to drive to New Orleans. I had made reservations to stay at the Hotel De La Poste. The hotel's desk clerk appeared to be literate, but you can never be too sure when dealing with a young creole sporting a moniker that reads "MabelRose." I paid for a week in advance and carried by own bags to room three twenty one. I considered getting some rest, but when you arrive in the French Quarter at ten in the evening, the only normal thing to do is enjoy the ambience of that space and time.

It started to rain and there's nothing like the Vieux Carre when a November thunderstorm pours out of that Louisiana sky. I walked with a red umbrella north on Charles Street past Royal and turned right onto Bourbon Street, heading east for three blocks to the corner of Saint Ann. I entered the River Shot Tavern. There were four rather nasty looking alcoholics, all white, looking mournful. The bartender seemed wired on a large quantity of thorazine or demerol—he was running at 33 1/3 in a world of 45 rpm. He had several tattoos, his arm read "Raised At Color Me Abused Daycare." Another arm read "Linda Lou's Dead." I wondered whether Linda Lou was his babysitter. I sure wasn't going to ask him about their genesis, creepy fuck might freak out on me. I ordered a long neck of Beck's. An old toothless greasy white man sitting to my immediate right spit a thick green yellow hocker between his legs directly on the old discolored wood floor. He peered at me through glaucoma scrimmed eyes and growled "That's been in there since '58."

"That was a good year," I told him. He turned away. I drank a total of five twelve ounce bottles and walked back to the hotel. It was still raining.

Before the elevator doors split open, MableRose came rushing out of her small cubicle with a message pad in hand.

"There was a long distance call for you." She pointed a long orange fingernail toward the bottom of the pink paper—"please return call. Toshiba Ushida" along with the number. I thanked Rose and handed her three one dollar bills which she tucked into her brassiere.

Inside the room overlooking a small water fountain, I packed a cigarette and with the help of AT&T was connected with the yellow man with all the money.

"Mr. Ball, so good to hear from you."

"Yes, you too Mr. Ushida." The jasmine slit eyed millionaire didn't waste any time getting to the heart of the matter.

"I take it you have in your possession the merchandise we negotiated in good faith."

"There's been a slight..."

"Mr. Ball, we know all about your failure to secure the materials in question."

"Well, ah…I am in possession of the…"

"I know quite well what you have in your possession. It does not impress me or my associates."

"BULLSHIT!" I hissed into the phone.

"Please act like a professional, like a business partner as we previously negotiated."

"Yes, but I'm in possession of the SK…"

"I know what's in your possession, Mr. Ball. Unfortunately it is not enough to complete the ritual. My syndicate contracted for the entire skeleton. Now that you have failed to secure the item we must rescind our original offer of two million American dollars. Do you understand?"

I bit hard on my lower lip, cutting the cigarette nearly in two. Tossing it into the ashtray and lighting another I thought THIS motherfucker was going to leave me hanging out to dry with the eight-ball head of Elvis Aaron. SON OF A BITCH! I had to play this cool, ICE cold.

"The skull is worth nothing to us without the other remains," he said, as if he were reading my thoughts.

"Look, Ushida. This is the KING'S head. The skull is circumscribed with sixteen metal staples that were used to fasten the cranial vault back together after the Memphis coroner removed the brain for tissue samples. IT'S ELVIS' HEAD GODDAMNIT!"

"Mr. Ball, I'm positively sure it is. We had the mansion under satellite surveillance. But it does not meet the specifications necessary for the ceremony, an observance and rite that must be adhered to. I can offer nothing."

"I KNOW WHAT THE FUCK YOU WANT BUT I CAN'T GO BACK TO GRACELAND, DO YOU UNDERSTAND?"

Ushida hated cursing, hated the disrespect and sloppiness that passed for English conversational language. I expected the phone to go dead any second. I was far from ice cold.

"Mr. Ball, control your emotions. You can solve this problem. May I suggest taking advantage of the fine library at Tulane University? Research the Ratchathani Ritual. You have one week to satisfy our demands. Goodnight."

"Ushida, wait." The phone went dead. BASTARD. What the fuck did he expect me to do? Going back to the mansion was out of the question, and what is research going to do for me? Christ! By now those Memphis boys had the leftovers on a whole new level of lockdown. Maybe that sick wetback fuck Lorga would take the skull off my hands. Shit. I would get raped. At the top end I would be lucky to see fifty thousand. How the hell was I going to survive on fifty dimes? I was sick. I went to fitful, troubled sleep.

The next morning I ate twenty four ounces of Alka-Seltzer and against my better judgment headed to Tulane University. I secured a visitor's pass and made a pass at a beautiful redhead student receptionist by the name of Carol Parker. She directed me to the fourth floor Quad C./Oriental Studies. The next seven hours were spent immersed in volumes of eastern sociology pertaining to Thailand, Cambodia, China, Vietnam, and Burma. Everything and nothing. Not a word anywhere about the Ratchathani Ritual. I had enough, said goodnight to Parker and headed back to the hotel for a cold twelve pack. I made a reservation at the Pelican Club and ate dinner alone.

For the next two days I continued my research to no avail. The only upside to all this wasted investigation was that mademoiselle Parker agreed to have dinner with me. On Thursday at noon as the library was becoming restless with starving undergraduates, I came upon a medium size pamphlet accidentally lodged inside a much larger tome. The essay was written by Dr. Dak Pax and was titled *The Secret History of Indonesian Ratchathani Observance*. The essay was forty five pages in length and held the secret to Ushida's riddle. With essay in hand I headed for the biographies. There were numerous biographies on the King of Rock and Roll and I started searching for that final piece of the supreme puzzle. The mystery waited on page sixty four of Albert Goldman's forgotten biography simply titled *Elvis*. I waited around for Parker and we drove into the French Quarter.

That evening we dine at K-Paul's on Chartres Street. Two entrees of Etouffe with cold draft beer. Parker was twenty-two, she was born in France, came to the states when she was six. Her mother Ruby Villerre fell in love with an American exchange student in Paris named Robert Thomas Parker. She became pregnant and six years later he sent for his unwed bride and child. They made New Orleans their home. After dinner, Parker stayed at the hotel. We did not make love.

In the morning I went down to the patio to read the local papers. Parker arrived a half hour later still damp from her morning shower. She looked absolutely ravishing wearing the same clothes as the day before, no makeup and damp red hair framing her white face resembling a Vermeer. We ate breakfast, ham and scrambled eggs, dry rye toast, and sipped chicory laced black coffee. I explained my immediate plans. She sipped her coffee and tugged lightly on a Virginia Slim. All I could think was Billy, don't fall in love.

"You're not going to believe this, but I have to drive to Mississippi to rob a grave."

"Anybody I know?" she asked in a mischievous, seductive tone.

"Maybe. Ever hear of Jesse Garon Presley?"

"That's Elvis' twin brother, right?"

"Yes."

"May I ask you why you want the remains of a stillborn baby?"

I put the Jack of Hearts face up on the table and began to tell her the whole burlesque story. She was elegant, savoring black coffee and dragging on those thin white cigarettes. "So you see, I can't go back to Graceland and this is where it gets a little weird with the occult. The Indonesian Syndicate would not purchase the skull, and my operative Mr. Ushida suggested I do some research on his favorite fetish. So I did. That's when I met you, doll."

"Now these mad freaks believe that if they consume the remains of the dead that they themselves become infused with the supernatural powers of the deceased. Now, since I'm not in possession of all the King's remains, the Ratchathani will accept as a substitute the remains of an identical twin. Exact DNA. This is where Jesse Garon comes into the picture. They'll obviously settle for the cadaver of the King's dead brother as a substitute for Elvis himself. As I explained earlier, I am in possession of the skull, which is the real corpse, and by midnight I hope to have proprietary rights to a small Buster Brown shoebox of precise DNA baby bones."

"When do we leave?"

"Now, doll."

I grabbed a few items from the hotel room and drove Parker to her apartment. I waited outside on Bienville Street as she threw some things together for the road trip. She mentioned mescaline. We headed north on the interstate 55 taking us past the Louisiana state line into Mississippi. It was all NORTH from there as the exits flew by like so many lost Confederate phantoms, all refrigerated white chalky typography on neon sage metal backgrounds measuring out the miles. McComb, Brookhaven, Crystal Springs, Jackson and further past Winona to Batesville where we headed to Tupelo. As late afternoon approached we slowly drifted past Elvis' birthplace which to the best of my defiled memory is East Tupelo. Idling the New Yorker up to an old Bell telephone booth, I stopped. I asked a young pale negro for directions to Princeville Cemetery. He stared back and said nothing from his shelter covered in bird shit. Three wrong turns and six dusk minutes later, we arrived.

To the right of the cemetery's entrance was a small well-kept red brick one room building occupied by a middle aged heavy metal Hispanic grave digger. He bore a striking resemblance to the Argentine revolutionary Che Guevara. He appeared half-baked from a prolonged use of inhalants. I introduced us as Doctor and Mrs. Parker, depression headstone researchers from the University of Mississippi, Hattiesburg. He spoke no English, and pointed to a registry on a simple wooden desk. He spoke in Spanish, and Parker spoke to him in French. He left the grounds in a black El Camino.

Parker opened the directory, thumbed through the dog-eared pages to the letter "P" and said "Jesse Garon Presley, unmarked, section (D4) plot 2."

It was now a simple matter of locating adjacent marked gravesites to pinpoint the final resting place of Elvis' older brother. Jesse was born dead thirty-five critical minutes before the little King's head was squeezed out from between Gladys' pelvic bones in a mad, primordial grunt.

Nursing a half-quart of cheap brown bourbon, we waited for nightfall. We spun several cassette sides of Elvis' greatest hits as the Mississippi sun hot faded into Arkansas. Eerie top forty, GO CAT GO!

Parker was trashed by the time I started the furtive exhumation. I shoveled the hard, rocky earth for what seemed like more than an hour when the metal blade made a dull thudding sound against a dry rotted pine box three feet deep. As I lifted the twenty inch carton out of its resting place, Parker, still alluring, staggered forward with flashlight in shaky hand. I could hear Elvis reverberating from the stereo inside the Chrysler, windows down.

"Oh LORD and MASTER of my life," she drunkenly howled. "Take from me the SPIRIT of SLOTH, DESPAIR, LUST of POWER and IDLE TALK!"

"Shut the fuck up," I whispered.

She was gone, fuckin' mescaline and bourbon, having a great time at my expense. She fell to her knees laughing in a pose of comic prostration.

"But GIVE rather the SPIRIT of CHASTITY, HUMILITY..."

"Parker, please."

"PATIENCE and LOVE...to your SERVANT."

Oh shit I thought, not again. Suddenly the still, black night was filled with the bawl, the wailing lament of several feral Mississippi hounds. "HOOOOOOOOOOO," they sang in unison.

"Parker, stop. This isn't fucking funny."

"Yes oh LORD and KING," she staggered to her feet. "GRANT me to SEEEEEE my own ERRORS and not to JUDGE my BROTHER!"

"Parker!" I shouted to no avail. We were going to get nailed.

"FOR YOU are BLESSED unto the AGES. The THIRD KING has risen!"

I cold cocked her. A right cross landing on her shapely chin. There were no teeth dislodged, I didn't break her jaw. There was no room to fuck this up. The hallucination sermon was over. I tossed Jesse's remains into the trunk and carried the knocked out mademoiselle into the back seat. I drove out of Tupelo with JUNG sitting on my right shoulder screaming UNBELIEVABLE NONSENSE.

Mad Arrivals

Mad, mad Chinamen will cross your polluted Atlantic salt waters and carry away your less than wholesome lunatic whores painted as Egyptian red concubines in the secret laboratories of your dead grandfather's ghost and dream. The flesh of all American women will become nuclear discharge for fifty-million blind and starving Pakistani's. Mao's revolutionary operas for the common man and class enemies are the only songs on the radio across Indiana highways toward Utah. The obese Mao waves his chrome plated automatic in the direction of your blond sister's cold cunt as the sky blue Mustang weaves toward the emperor Gilmore. The white assassin.

The Mao-Man is now huge, his bright yellow flesh molded into the leather bucket seats while his hand shakes his little red book out the windshield, steering and shifting with the steady, fat green long-nailed opposite hand. Indiana State Troopers stand silent along the defeated asphalt, only their sad squad car lights emit any semblance of a past holy America. An America that was proud and greedy destroyed by the frozen sperm of their President, gun the motor flown to Finland where he shall lick and suck the dirty strawberry colored pussy of his teenage lust with Hewlett-Packard slush fund at the ready. Poor star. Poor stripe. Let the children play. No.

The gone ghost god Gilmore waits with blond head bent toward the new rainbow of his fashionable Europe. He carries cigarettes and compact discs. At the Mao-Man's request he has no luggage. The Ford screeches and smokes in front of the plastic concrete prison. Gilmore crawls over the weight of his new King and from the back seat squirms his thin pink tongue into Chinese hair lip past off white teeth. The Mao-Man lets out the clutch and the Ford flies into the darkness of the new republic.

Dawn. The Nevada desert where the neon never sleeps. Drunken Japanese gamblers stray out of lost broken casino dreams and weave past the blistered parked Mustang. The Mao-Man slurps on twelve vanilla milkshakes. Gilmore has a fourteen year old Baptist virgin on her knees sucking his new prince Clinton dick, his first hetero blow job since his execution. He does not violate her Pope love hole, Gilmore is a gentleman. The parents watch from cold closed circuit television inside the MGM Grand. When Gilmore shoots, digital cameras record the event. A New World. Forget that pimp hump Huxley and that bald fat fucker Caesar, this is a new dimension.

Gilmore slaps the young protestant lass on her blue jean clad ass and sends her in the direction of the second government. The Two D.D.G. Located in close proximity to the MGM Grand Sports Book. The bartender pours drinks. He sports an automatic rifle on his left shoulder. He has been holy cleared to carry weapons of immense destruction while in the presence of the New Two. And why not? The helicopter used in five presidential administrations featured a 70's olive green shag chair emblazoned with the presidential seal, behind that chair another olive green shag chair next to a red phone and a briefcase attached to the wall containing all the nuclear codes. Behind that, a liquor cabinet. Let's launch the codes, and here's to first of the day. The New Two. See, now there are two governments in past America. The Two D.D.G. and The TWO. The TWO being Mao and Gilmore, like launch codes and booze, like bullets and guns. The Two D.D.G. is what the wizard Mao left in his fission wake to appease all new slave Croats. The burnt red nuclear glow of the House of Representatives got a Congress of Black Magic Women.

A painting cannot be reproduced too much, as say a recording is played in excess, to the point where it loses its magic. There is no saturation point. The essence is removed from continual hearing but not from continuous reproduction and or viewing. A reproduction possesses no presence unless that reproduction is an original. Also, when the artist is not in the act of painting, the painter still paints, but with a different medium.

July 7, 1971.

Beautifully fat and high and poetic.

Bathed in warm blue bathwater.

Empty whiskey bottles sleep.

Jim Morrison est mort!

Freedom of information is an oxymoron wrapped inside an affront. When she was a child there were no interpreters, only copycats. White blues artists singing in the Whiskey and LSD nightclubs of California. Long playing albums contained a pop spirituality for those inclined to lean in that direction. These vinyl icons are the black oil explosion and debris trail of the screaming comet that was rock and roll music. Now come over here. Take your panties off. I got to get a grip. She laughed like Eric Burdon. Fade back to the roof top, freeze it, roll the credits.

Masterson stretched sheer white panty hose over her hips, threw her dress over her head and ran for the yellow bus. She began to bleed and crossed her long legs. Some men take to the scent of menstruation like a shark to pork chops. Once she was hiking while on her period and got attacked by two dogs. That scent amounted to some kind of threat, always does. She placed her dark panes over her eyes. Everything in her field of vision turned blue.

"Your mother killed herself."

"She was dead years ago."

"She stuck her head in an oven."

"She never could cook."

Masterson had a better understanding of the self she wants to mangle; the ego that was created by parent, school, church, and country. She wore great transforming outerwear to emerge from herself and distance these ghost selves from all others. She read Rimbaud and Superman. She saw something scurrying across the floor of the bus, a shadow in her eye's corner. "More tea, waiter," I said. And what will the gentleman be having for breakfast? "Pig's blood and two cigars, I'm expecting a priest." The waiter asked if I would like a gun. I told him I already had one. He smiled and walked into the kitchen. Then came the horrible shriek of the suckling, and a rush of red clamor from behind smudged aluminum doors. They brought fresh flowers to the table. A morning paper. I glanced at the television and felt the familiar disgust and loathing that comes with the cultural download that is the daily news. This is what's happening. No, it isn't. The warm pig's blood arrives, and I ask for black pepper. A second beverage is offered, cold goat's milk over ice. I decline. Mother's milk is poison. He arrives with the cigars and shows me a digital picture of tonight's entree. Morrison Clown asked me if I remembered that song Mr. Flashback use to sing. "You remember Billy, he was screaming down the street fully loaded both in mind and automatic weapon."

"The school children named him Mr. Flashback, he was 52 years old, white and as nuts as President Reagan."

"I thought you liked Ronald Reagan!"

"I do, but that doesn't change the fact that he's loonier than

Hunter Thompson on a free fist full of E. and two chilled bottles of
champagne."

The Superstition Song
Beware of government snipers
Infants baptized in dirty water
The uneducated Christian centurion
Starving dark skinned children
Crack whores in withdrawal
Liars, pimps, priests and politicians
That sticky hole in her derriere
New green money
Hospitals, whole eggs and milk
Illiterate rappers from Cleveland
Cable television and soiled yellow panties
Religious zealots
Old books with red ink falsifications
A girl with no face
And women who ovulate

ELEVEN

It was unseasonably cool as the Chrysler streaked through the fog shrouded Mississippi night. Jesse was huddled in the trunk with his young brother's cranium. Parker was out cold in the back seat; her short denim skirt struggled to cover the cool cheeks of her bottom. I did not play the radio. I did not play any cassettes. No music at all. I was trying to clear my consciousness. That last play ball affliction damn near sent me over the edge. I kept a watchful eye on the four lanes and rehearsed my negotiation strategy with Ushida. He would play hardball. I would hold fast at one million even, would start the transaction at a million four. I thought about Parker. The nerve-racking flipped out French ballerina locked up and strip searched in the squalor of a Tupelo jail house. We were lucky.

As I maneuvered four steel belt Firestone radials through Holly Springs National Forest, Parker attacked from the back seat. JESUS CHRIST! She leaped on my head and started to pummel me, grabbed my ponytail and started to choke me. My vision was totally obscured as the Fifth Avenue veered left then heaved precariously to the right engaging the soft gravel shoulder. She started to scream obscenities at eardrum bursting decibels. She was now hanging on top of my head and the air in my lungs became hot with the first signs of hyperventilation. In a near panic I smashed the brakes and we careened along the roadway in a nauseating sideways bent. The Chrysler came to an abrupt stop. I was slumped over the steering column as my monster mademoiselle continued her assault. I took several vicious blows to the right ear and one smart smack to the throat, all the while strapped in by the safety belt. I would have to kill her to get her off of me.

I reached behind the red leather seat with my free right arm and yanked her over the front seat into the dashboard. I released the seatbelt, took the keys from the ignition and exited, leaving the door open. Gasping for air, I did the only normal thing I could think of, walking up the interstate and lighting a Marlboro waiting to see if the mother rat was going to attack AGAIN. What a fucking nightmare. This wasn't bourbon poisoning. I took a hot drag on the cigarette.

Parker stumbled out of the driver's side door and landed on her ass. I didn't dare laugh. Her blue eyes were on fire with rage and her pink fingernail clenched fists were positioned to strike.

"Just hold it," I pleaded. Then she went off like an exploding roman candle. I back tracked with my hands above my head in a gesture of surrender. "Relax, Parker. Relax." She was ten feet away from me. Her appearance reflected in the fog and yellow moonlight showed how disheveled she appeared, her white sweater torn exposing a pink pushup bra and her denim skirt rode high into the crack of her ass revealing long bare legs. One of her high heels had broken off and she stood unbalanced. "You think this is funny, asshole?"

"No, this is not funny." I cracked. Too late, lost it. In fact if she'd had a revolver strapped to her sexy thigh, she would have shot.

"I'll kill you, cocksucker," she shrieked. Retrieving the empty bottle of booze, she hurled it at me as I retreated north on I 55. Several cars flew by flashing their headlamps. She missed. BANG!

"Look, you had a little too much to drink, a bad tab of mesc. I'm sorry. Hey, I don't know, you could have got us arrested in Mississippi for grave robbing."

"Come over here now!"

"No fucking way, lady."

"You chickenshit!" she mumbled disgustedly and walked away.

I waited fifteen minutes chain smoking before I took a seat behind the wheel. Parker was now sitting in front. I turned the ignition and glided back onto the four lanes. Not one word of conversation was exchanged as we headed south. She was still seething as we pulled into the parking garage of the Hotel De La Poste. Parker exited and slammed the door. She opened the rear door and retrieved her garment bag. She began to walk barefoot through the garage, clutching her bag and high heels to her breasts. Christ, she was beautiful.

"I'll pick you up at eight for dinner. Pelican Club?"

She spun around on her bare feet and said "Go FUCK yourself!"

"I'll make a later reservation if eight is an inconvenience."

She made a left turn out of the garage. I was falling for her. I headed for the elevators and rode three floors, entered, secured the door, and landed on the bed fully clothed.

The Dream

Welcome to Hell. The King has been slain by an overweight offensive lineman from the Green Bay Packers. Not too many people know of this wretched tragedy. Mr. Presley was hailing a cab on the corner of Fourth and State when Otis Marshall, wacked on cheap red wine and white trash New Jersey gash, reached into his Vaseline blotched orange Walmart parka and slowly fired six rounds of hollow point lead into Mr. Presley's back.

The cab driver, Mr. Luis 'Greasy Dick' Rojas stated "The King never knew what happened." Rojas later stated at the Neville County Police Station that Presley's last words were "Jesse, Jesse Garon was murdered at birth, uh, because...he was a black twin." Then Presley spilled legs akimbo onto a yellow urine soaked cardboard box.

Two big busted wet pussy juveniles also witnessed the assassination. They filed police reports stating that Otis Marshall exposed himself to three elderly Catholic Nuns before squeezing off the fatal shots.

The girls claim that the assassin pulled out his thick deformed cock with his left hand and jerked himself to an unholy African climax screaming "Chuck Berry is the King, you dirty piece of Memphis dog shit."

To further complicate the witness testimony, enter one unemployed bartender named Rudy Clemente who had just arrived in the cheese state from a rat and crack infested barrio in East Los Angeles. Rudy states that two days earlier he overheard the assassin mumbling to himself that Elvis was selling photographs of Marshall's sixteen year old daughter fornicating with a large albino crocodile named Pete.

According to Mr. Clemente, "See, it was not the fact that Elvis was a latent pornographer, but that the crocodile had been a virgin since birth, and that Marshall rescued the young reptile from a family of starving North Vietnamese refugees."

Thirteen months later in a Wisconsin courtroom, Clemente would testify that the brutal murder of the greatest singer in the short history of recorded music was in part an attempted cover up. Clemente cried as he testified. "See, Mr. Presley tried to eat all the incriminating evidence. He tried to stuff a half dozen eight by ten inch glossies down his throat with six Chiquita bananas." Clemente then pantomimes the last frantic moments of *the King. The twelve jurors were aghast and the judge called for Pepto-Bismol and immediate recess.*

When the court reconvened, one of the sisters who had been violated by the vision of cock and subsequent ejaculation reached under her habit and pulled out a Charter Luger. She strafed the courtroom; she killed the defendant and his three Chicano attorneys. Then she put the automatic into her creepy crooked mouth and blew the left side of her cranial vault completely off. Seconds later, the ghost of Elvis appeared, the handsome '68 Special leather Elvis, and spewed black and white photo fragments mixed with partially digested banana upon the dead sister's corpse. The court stenographer committed suicide by inhaling two grams of Comet, the stain remover.

Within minutes, eight dark blue and pearly white squad cars screeched to a halt outside the courthouse. Police Chief Doug Dawson blew into the courtroom and started barking out orders while clutching a fifth of dry vermouth and finger-fucking a fourteen year old blind Puerto Rican girl. The young girl jabbered in Spanish as she clutched her breasts and moaned with pleasure toward anyone who dared look in the Chief's direction. She smiled revealing shards of green teeth. Having satisfied himself, the Chief removed his fat nail-bitten hand from the girl's snatch and she ran out of the courtroom blowing kisses of dental decay.

Then a detective Harrison came crashing into the courtroom clutching a bright yellow Western union Telegraph in one hand and dragging a known Japanese homosexual named Jimmy Wang. Harrison quietly spoke with the Chief out of earshot of the other officers. "That's right, Chief. I was shaking this Wang fag down on a solicitation charge when he decided to cop a plea in front of District Attorney Gail Goodhump. He said he knew the nun was going to go psycho, but was afraid to report it."

"Speak you miserable jaundiced dick eater." Jimmy Wang was visibly shaken. Before he could mumble another broken syllable, Chief Dawson cracked him in the mouth with his flashlight. Jimmy slumped to the marble floor where the Chief clubbed him again on the back of his bald head and he was out cold for the next hour. Several Madison Tribune journalists hauled the stupefied Wang into the Judge's chambers and tried to have their way with his passed out ass, only to be shot by another angry nun. Shit, they were everywhere.

Detective Harrison showed the telegraph to the Chief. Dawson mumbled some obscenities and had the message shredded. The Chief shook his head in disbelief and said "I can't believe this shit. The telegram was from the Vatican, Papal Headquarters." Harrison lost his amused look. "That's right, the Pope himself, the Big Dog of organized religion. God's representative in a dress. The spiritual quarterback of millions. Christ, I get the feeling we're going to be up to our asses in Catholics before nightfall."

The Chief and several of his officers were visibly intoxicated when American Airlines flight 909 touched down on the grey rain soaked tarmac of Neville County Airport. Six bald and bearded priests were flown in from Rome. They proceeded to the courthouse without escort. The holy men remained silent during their ten minute commute. When they arrived they were accosted by four Latino gangsters offering deviant sexual gratification and an array of illegal drugs. They brushed aside the greasy punks and the holy men arrived at the scene of the murder and Elvis ghost sighting.

By now, Chief Dawson was smashed to the gills and belligerent as a heretic. One of the priests looked at the Chief with disgust, silently covering himself with the sign of the Holy Cross. The Chief backed off in cowardly reverence.

Then, WHAM. A small flask of holy water was poured directly onto the site where the suicidal sister collapsed.

"God in Heaven have mercy!" screamed the Chief.

When that holy water hit the floor, all Hell broke loose.

A three foot Norwegian midget appeared, dressed and looking very much like a parody of Elvis' manager, Colonel Tom. The dwarf look alike began spinning counter clockwise and pleading with the holy men to sign exclusive recording contracts. Suddenly, three dozen yellow canaries flew out from the inside of the midget's yellow sport coat lining and perched themselves on the courtroom bench. The birds began harmonizing a quasi-rendition of "Don't Be Cruel."

Chief Dawson had seen enough. Drunkenly, he pulled his magnum from its holster and began blasting the little bastard and his birds. Contractual papers and feathers littered the courtroom mixing with the phantom photo scraps and masticated banana of the Elvis ghost. The smoke cleared and the King's mother appeared. It was Gladys. She brandished a Russian AK47. She was pissed.

Dawson fired round after round after round. A white lightning bolt shot out of Gladys' left eye and the Chief's head went up in flames. The remaining law enforcement officers were dumbstruck. Detective Harrison drew his revolver much too late. Gladys strafed the Detective with the AK47 and he was no more. Two of the priests had passed out from satanic fear, and the other holy men clasped hands and began to chant in unison "That's all right now Mama."

I was looking from the left and it occurred to me as I watched a cockroach crawl across the floor of the courtroom that I was lucid dreaming. The second I became aware of this, the cockroach stopped and seemed to look at me directly.

"Hey," I thought I heard the cockroach say to me though it was impossible. I was hearing this in my head. Then it hit me -- ropes of ejaculate were draped over his antennae like a sick halo or crown. Christ, it was the cockroach from Graceland, still covered in Diamond Dog's spent load. Wake me up from this, someone.

"You won't wake up, not yet." The Graceland cockroach scurried over to me and continued. "I couldn't go back to the hive.

The neurological damage from the insecticide I ate caused me to forget where I originally lived."

"I guess it's a coincidence we've met again," I said, and the intense gravity of the dream space logic suddenly made this telepathy between me and the insect the most important conversation I'd ever have in my life. "I can't go back there either, for different reasons."

"We're both in exile, Billy," he tapped the courtroom floor. "I'm sending messages. Now I report my travels back to whomever can pick up these frequencies I communicate with these tappings. My pheromones can't be picked up now since your dear acquaintance gave me this condition, but I can still use percussion and interpretive dance to talk to the ones I'll never see again."

"Please, tell me what you're saying to them," I blurted out, surprised by the urgency in my own voice.

"I've become an entertainer. I interpret contemporary pop songs. Dominic Ierace's Love Is Like A Rock. The J. Geils Band's Love Stinks. I've managed to relay in my own simple way the absurdity of reproduction and the certainty of our demise."

The Graceland Roach had me under a spell. I needed answers. "How do you know anyone can hear you? What...what should I do, I have to get out of here, I..."

"Billy. Shut up. You won't figure out anything. Everything is just going to happen to you and you'll deal with it. How do I know the hive can hear me? Learn to be heard by your own species and we'll talk." He scurried under a chair next to me, Diamond

112

Dog's opaque ropes trembling on his antenna. Suddenly he spun around, creeping forward into the courtroom light and said "You'll wake up soon, but it's still going to be a nightmare. Piece of shit human."

The Graceland cockroach's spell over me was broken, and I was no longer a participant in my dream. I went back to a kind of third person omnipresent observation of this movie that wouldn't stop. Later in the afternoon, a hail of large cockroaches pelted Graceland. Vernon Presley spoke to a local Memphis news reporter. "I don't know anything," groaned Vernon. "This is all Examiner bullshat."

Claudia Maddux, a veteran war correspondent, states that Vernon Presley has no knowledge of the alleged sighting of his son or the preposterous reincarnation of his deceased wife Gladys.

Ms. Maddux continues to press Vernon on recent allegations that he is in fact not the father of the King, and that Jesse was killed at birth because he was a negro bastard child. In other words, Vernon, your late wife Gladys was banging some nigger in Florida while you were drunk on cheap Tennessee Gin, chasing and sniffing after your brother's daughter all around Tupelo with an infected pink ofay hard-on. "Care to comment?"

"Now Miss Maddux, everyone knows I'm Elvis' father, and his brother was stillborn at death. At birth, for that matter. You know what I mean. And with that I'd like you goddamn camera carrying fucks to leave the hallowed grounds of Graceland."

"*I'm coming with the gun, Vernon,*" *threatened Grandma.*

It did not matter that the interview was a dead end. The can of southern worms was opened. All the major news networks carried the live feed and history was forever changed by the pale white flat chested Episcopalian reporter walking away, high heels crunching through the cockroach field caused by that Old Testament hailstorm.

Two days later. It has been reported that Vernon Presley bought two one-way airline tickets to Paraguay. This also coincides with the disappearance of a twelve year old Nashville girl, Gloria Miller, one of only three females in existence to have a rare congenital birth defect known as Siamese Vaginata. A lass born with two twats. Oh, Vernon!

Interpol was notified the next day and the Paraguayan Secret Police were briefed that evening. As of that following Tuesday, the authorities in the south central South American country stated that it appears that Presley and the young circus sideshow freak of nature slipped into the agrarian homeland undetected.

A week later, flight attendant Isabel Juarez stated to the Central Intelligence Agency that "a strange white haired old man, sitting in first class on flight 023, kept grunting and smelling his fingers throughout the flight." It was too late. VANISHED.

TWELVE

YOUR CHRIST! I woke up in a cold sweat. My clothes were soaked through to the sheets. What a nightmare. I stared at the orange neon digital readout of a Magnavox electronic clock radio as I slowly re-acclimated to reality. Six PM. I rolled out of bed, stripped off the wet clothes. Smoked a cigarette on the toilet, naked. As I stood showering under the filthiest tap water in the continental United States, a hurricane force message from the almighty skull reader appeared. *You Can't Do That*, the Beatles wrote that song about New Orleans tap water, don't swallow it.

I dried off and tossed on a black sweater and a pair of black jeans, no socks. I turned on the television, no sound, the glow from a different light year. A barrage of murder, death, destruction, inhumanity, ethnic cleansing, genocide, rape, mayhem, corruption, desolation, graft, greed, disasters, disease, addiction...and these were just the commercials. An anesthetic aesthetic cathode ray tube of pulsating cool blue bits of worthless attempts at communication and disinformation flickered across my optic nerves in candy-colored waves of brainwashed grain, processed and categorized into the pattern recognition generator that is the human brain, parts placed on predictable shelves of memory.

I grabbed an open twelve ounces of warm bottled Beck's and flung it at the television. The bottle appeared to smack Bernard Shaw on his nappy shell-shocked head. He appeared to careen from side to side as the green carafe spun out of control on top of the dresser drawer. I called Parker. She slammed the phone down when she heard my voice. I called again, same result. I stopped calling.

I dined at the Pelican Club alone, a rack of lamb, rare, wild rice, red house wine, Turkish coffee and cigarettes for dessert. I charged it to my American Express. Later, I walked slowly through a late October sky. Alone.

I entered the Blue Sax. There was a $15 cover charge, and Buddy Guy live in concert. A wall of thunderous heat and roar of not one but two electric lead guitars rumbled through the small club as I worked my way toward the rear. Guy was doing a cover of Little Richard's "True Fine Mama." The joint was a high tension two hundred and twenty volt blow out. Guy was trying to detonate Louisiana. His guitar was incandescent, he could split atoms. My ears were scalded. Magnificent. I kept my panes on throughout the night, drank import. Guy damn near went through his entire repertoire. He bent the evening in half like a lawless nuclear warhead and then it was over.

I took my time walking back through the French Quarter. The night was illuminated with a thousand Van Gogh stars, the reincarnation of Johannes Kepler.

The next morning I spoke with Toshiba Ushida. The negotiations were fierce and criminal. I maintained a professional demeanor and understood his position on renegotiations, a half hour transatlantic phone call. It was settled. One million U.S. Dollars. The exchange would take place in Las Vegas, Nevada. Ushida arranged everything, plane tickets. Two in case Parker wanted to travel with me. Probably not. One of his operatives would meet me at the airport, at the entrance next to the Continental Sky Caps. Fake identification would be provided. Ushida requested that the remains should not be checked in with the luggage. I was to carry them through security and onto the plane. If stopped by security I was an assistant coroner carrying remains of a homicide back to Las Vegas for forensic testing. Dr. William Ball.

In the afternoon I had lunch at Tujaques, the house specialty, corned beef and boiled cabbage. Later I purchased a silver attaché case. From a pay phone I leave several messages on Parker's answering machine.

Walking along Bourbon Street around five in the afternoon I decided to have a couple of beers and shoot some pool. The red neon says FIREHOUSE BAR and GRILL. I ordered two long necks of Miller and slipped four quarters into the pay table. I rack – CRACK – and fifteen colored spheres were set in chaotic motion. The red three ball careened into the left side pocket. The purple four exited and disappeared into the far right corner, and the white cue ball flew off the table and landed with a thunk, a sad abortion humming along moody marred wood planking. I retrieved it and proceed to run the table. Several hours passed in this manner, and I left another message with my pissed off mademoiselle. I explain that I'm flying to Las Vegas and I have a seat reserved for her. I leave; bought a large take-out pizza with everything – hold the hairy fish.

Inside I showered, dressed in a black polo shirt, long sleeves, blue Levi's, no underwear, no socks. I turned the Panasonic bastard box on the X Channel with hosts Hard Rod Randolph and Petula Slickdiamond. Only in LOOOOSIANA.

The phone rang and it was Parker. She was in the lobby and asked if she could come up.

"Of course."

I left the door ajar and waited two breathless minutes and in she walked. She was wearing a red sweater and tight blue jeans. White Reebok walking shoes without socks. I kissed her gently on the forehead, took her hands in mine and attempted to apologize. She stuck her tongue in my mouth.

"You taste like pizza."

"You taste like Scope."

"Not for long." She helped herself to a slice.

"Pour me a glass of wine, Billy, these jeans are killing me." She kicked off her shoes, still laced. Then she removed her jeans. She was wearing opaque blue panties, evocative of a precise shadow. She propped two pillows against the headboard. She was the most beautiful woman I'd ever seen.

"What are we watching?"

"Ah, the X Channel." I am slightly embarrassed.

"Do you believe this?"

"It's the bleak future of television."

"Oh my Lord, this is sick," Parker screeched with delight.

"This is Marshall McLuhan with an erection."

"Oh God Billy this is perverted."

"Yes."

"What's he doing with the CAT? Oh no Billy, please change the channel."

"No wait, please, check this out."

"AHHHH He's going to ejaculate on that poor kitty."

"No he's not."

"That asshole's a degenerate. Please turn it off, please!" Parker covered her blue eyes and kicked her feet like a school girl. "Billy is it over?"

Suddenly the screen blanked into an atomic shade of turquoise. I caught Parker peeking through her fingers.

"See, they don't show the explosion."

"Thank GOD. Turn it off, turn it off."

The screen remained blank for about thirty seconds and then Petula Slickdiamond appeared, naked, except for an LSU football helmet perched on her head. She was seated on a porcelain toilet bowl, legs splayed. She brandished a seven inch green cucumber. "Welcome to the green grocer portion of our show." The small live studio audience applauded.

"No WAY." Parker said.

"SHHHH."

"Now when inserting a large farm product into your love hole, you must be absolutely sure to use one of our recommended lubricants. Hellman's Mayonnaise works especially well when trying to insert one of nature's own dildos up your tempting tunnel."

"She didn't just say that."

"Watch."

Then Slickdiamond wiped a large gob of antique white dressing onto half the length of the fleshy gourd and introduced the mess into her quivering urn.

"Nooooo!" Shrieked Parker.

As soon as Slickdiamond slid that happy tendril halfway up her snatch, she passed feminine wind into the highly sensitive audio microphones. I nearly cried from laughter. Parker was incredulous. Slickdiamond slid the cucumber in and out in a furious motion. Again the screen went blank and we both convulsed in uncontrollable laughter. I turned the television OFF.

Parker kissed me passionately on the mouth. She then confessed that she was still a virgin – unexperienced in matters of sex. I told her not to worry. I would teach her...slowly. We kissed, laughed, hugged, drank wine and fondled each other like teenagers. I was falling in love with her, and she awoke on Saturday morning still a virgin.

I showered, shaved, dressed and asked Parker to do the same. She was ill, too much wine. I pleaded with her that we were going to miss the flight. "Get your beautiful ass out of that bed now!"

"Go away Billy, please."

I turned on the shower and yanked her out of bed. I had her sweater in my left hand and grabbed the back of her panties with my right and marched her clothed into the rusty hotel rainfall. She cursed in French and I closed the door. I ordered breakfast from room service. Her red wet sweater and soaked panties flew out of the bathroom and landed in puddles at my feet. She dressed, we ate, and took a cab to the airport.

THIRTEEN

Exiting the cab in front of the Continental entrance, we were greeted by a nameless operative. He handed me the documents, left, Parker hanging onto my right arm. I left one suitcase with the Skycap, carried the contraband in the silver attaché and approached security. Parker placed her black leather bag on the conveyor and walked through the metal detector. I placed the attaché on the conveyor and followed. Nothing. No security check. Amazing. We arrived at Gate D17 and within the hour we displayed our boarding passes. Parker had the window, I had the aisle. First Class. We declined the champagne and within a half hour we were cruising at thirty six thousand feet. There was an unimpeachable feeling of discomfort, a cold convalescence. I was numb as I realized there's no escape from catastrophe. This heretic of the mind becomes hyper-phobic amongst sudden turbulence. Passengers silently articulate the sign of the cross. That pathetic pantomime with not save you, I think to myself. DOOM is DOOM. And no amount of blind faith will prevent you from being annihilated.

Parker had fallen asleep. Curled in a blanket of blue. A Parisian Princess. I read the USA Today sports page. We arrived in the biggest whorehouse on earth at approximately 12 pm. Pacific Time. Forty college football games were available for wagering. Another fifteen professional contests available on Sunday. Decadence beyond any Biblical Golden Calf. One million bloody hammers awaited the addicted and beyond the horror hype and narcotic neon glow of a United States Federal Bankruptcy Court, the most prolific in the Union. A scathing indictment. Capitalistic desertification.

Parker slept through the landing, we came in hot and low. Had to have scorched the white roofs of taxi cabs. The engines whined and pleaded and the tires and brakes petitioned the pilot for clemency. A few passengers applauded our safe arrival.

We were first to deplane. Walking briskly through the gloom of McCarran Airport, we escalated down toward our solo suitcase already spinning on the carousel. An MGM Grand limousine waited with female chauffeur. Within minutes we arrived, checked into a suite then headed directly to Ushida's massive suite. The transaction was fast and hospitable. We exchanged attaché cases. Ushida did not check its contents and I didn't check mine. We toasted with hot sake. It is over.

We elevator down. A million dollars rich. The money was placed in an MGM vault. I signed all required documents. We retired to our suite. Secured the door. Parker showered first. I ordered two bottles of chilled Mondavi Chenin Blanc. They arrived in two faux silver holders, two wine glasses included and a corkscrew. I showered next, a slow languid rain.

Parker sat on the king size bed. She had opened and poured the wine. I joined her on the bed, a dry towel wrapped around my wet frame. We raised glasses.

"Congratulations, Billy."

"Thanks, Parker." We took huge gulps of wine and laughed…together. Sitting across from me, her white legs rested across my thighs. We began to make love, a slow river of new sex. I raised her black garment and her breasts appeared in front of my eyes, two soft marbles. We kissed. Her red hair now tangled, covering her cobalt eyes. She was radiant, spiritual light. An infinite ideal. She dazzled.

"Are you God?"

"No."

She removed the towel, I was a flesh jacket – long, erect, a Caravaggio.

"You have a beautiful cock."

I removed her panties, she was not naked…she was nude. I licked all her watercolor box painted toes. I placed my tongue in her raspberry mouth. It evoked new blood. Her eyes were candlelight. She is Egyptian. Her skin became translucent. She sat delicately upon me. All grace…aura. She is viscous fur, an exotic animal, she rides silk. She was deflowered. Liquid watermelon glaze tainted the sheets. This was no conquest, this was spiritual fusion. The Countess upon her surrender. Your pop culture came to a standstill. I could not let the ghost of my semen invade. The ejaculate lay elegantly upon her. I ate it.

"The Sun is GOD, Billy!"

"That just didn't happen, she didn't say any of that," Masterson offered.

"What didn't happen?"

Masterson, in the year 2024, seemed more skeptical of me than ever, especially of this story.

The Television's amplified volume in this hotel bar mocked my question by stepping on our conversation with my own words. "What did happen?" The announcer, square and middle aged, sported thick black glasses with slightly smudged lenses that matched his disheveled middle aged appearance. He speculated. "What happened to Candy? What exactly happens when pop stars evolve? Well, I'll tell you. We've followed her story and her rise to pop stardom is known to all of us. She's the one true daughter of God. She realized, in Wichita, Kansas after a peyote ritual with Bach's Brandenburg Concerto as a soundtrack, our Candy realized that God was just another man to be scorned. The pop music bubble - well, popped! Her third eye opened. Candy rejected her Christgirl pop destiny through denial of THE FATHER by changing her sound, her look and her marketing line. We're all familiar with her hit making reggae band full of disdain for capitalism and God. Enter today's number 1 Billboard hit, *'Your Dog's on LSD'* How much fun is it that we all get to be a part of Candy's rebellion against GOD - DOG on LSD, complete with her amazing dreadlocks, spliff and Rasta stylings..." The announcer made his point by lighting a Cheech and Chong sized joint on camera, a camera that then zoomed in slowly on the rolling paper, twisted into shape and covered with a colorful repetitive motif of a dog's head and print that read DOG GOD in a festive pattern. The Candy brand was everywhere, her omnipresence through marketing more complete than Daddy God's eternal efforts at being ALL THINGS. She was the great I AM.

"She never said 'You have a beautiful cock'. No woman would say that to a man. As far as asking if you're God, well," Masterson pointed to the TV and laughed, less like a laugh than a high pitched squeal. "I wish Candy were here to listen to this! I'd like to see you point your Caravaggio cock at HER!"

I stared blankly at the TV screen, not in the mood to argue with Masterson when she said "But you don't need ME to be your Sherpa guide to the Palace of Bad Decisions."

And there it was on the sports bar TV, Candy's hit video, *Your Dog's on LSD*.

Flew in from Iraq
With a head full of THC

Blood and sand and body parts

Sadr city memories

I saw my bookie on a color TV

He said you owe four dimes

And your dog's on LSD

Sunday morning, hurling a BLT

I said to the fat man

Give me Detroit and three

Spoke with your attorney

Skinny St. Katie

She said you was crazy

And your dog's on LSD

I got no power

No electricity

She's always splaying

Caucasian indecency

That nasty white chick

Took a chainsaw to my knee

I knew I was shell shocked

And your dog's on LSD

In Mississippi

They eat their young for free

The women are black and cheap

A confederate STD

Last week I saw my doctors

The hermaphrodites Grant and Lee
They scheduled a lobotomy and said
Your dog's on LSD

The music was so loud I nearly missed her leaning in and shouting to me "You don't always remember things correctly, Billy."

"Explain."

"That time you left me in the tub and got in the cab? The day I paid you back? I wasn't crying and reaching out for you like you tell everyone. I dropped my fucking contact lens on the bathroom floor. I needed your help. Egomaniac!"

"Come on, I know what happened, I was there!"

"She never said you have a beautiful cock. I'm too versed in your fiction style to buy into your story. Not a plausible scenario. I can prove it."

"How?"

"A survey." Masterson got out her smart phone. While she frantically text messaged, the ambient light from the bar illuminated her golden hair that hung over her face in forgotten tangles. She was getting to me.

"What survey, tell me."

"I'm group texting my ex boyfriends to see if anyone ever told them they had a beautiful cock."

I put my head down on the bar and sighed. "What's this

going to prove?"

"Plausibility. Just wait. We have to wait for them to answer."

The waitresses, dressed like extras from *Laugh In*, carried shots of whiskey in tall lime green florescent tubes on mother of pearl trays. Placed in front of me, I said why not? The music these days had taken a turn -- the opposite of 70's rock misogyny, sexism turned in on itself. In the future world women were on top and men were servants. A few oldies still fit in -- a Sparks tune from 1974 began with a loud jolt. *At Home, At Work, At Play...* Masterson was right next to me but we may as well have been miles apart, parallel lines of opinion that'd never intersect like our beliefs once did, like our lives once did, like our bodies once did. *I'm gonna love you under incandescent light, I'm gonna love you under the florescent light...* I slowly examined and turned my thin glowing green shaft of a shot and listened. *She's unique especially at home where you're butler, maid and often cook....*

"Shit!" Hunched over, Masterson's face was illuminated by the white light rectangle of her phone. She'd been madly texting, and now she was scowling. "Shit, shit shit. It wasn't supposed to go down this way, so to speak." She laughed despite her humiliation upon discovering from an old lover that she'd said, in a moment of passion, the very thing she'd declared impossible. "I can't BELIEVE I told Steve he had a beautiful cock!"

I hung my head in a fit of giggles and finally had to stop to ask "Does he remember the past correctly?"

She threw her phone in her purse in disgust. "Yes," she moaned. "Never caught him in a lie. Totally honest. What a schmuck."

Or at play between the tennis sets,
Or at play before she's placed her bet
Or at play while she's still slightly wet
Or at play while she is dripping wet
At Home, At Work, At Play....

That was before she became a nun. Yes, Masterson. I couldn't help but wonder if that night was part of some kind of impetus or realization leading to this drastic change of life for a woman who was once an amazing creature of physical pleasure. Eroticism is a fragile ecosystem of fantasy avoiding too much reality. We had too much reality. I understood, or thought I did, because I was done, too. Almost done with Screams From The Balcony, almost done with heart shaped asses, almost done with white negroes, almost done with the George Shearing Quintet, almost done with cold air and hot cigarettes, almost done with politics and media, almost done with food, almost done with choking the chicken, almost done with walks and foolish shoes, almost done with televised light and opaque thigh highs, almost done with violas and violets, almost done with cops and judges and shamans, almost done with almost done.

Masterson's Soliloquy

Being a nun in this era, well, it's a different gig. We don't have to be married to Christ. Les Chants de Maldoror by Comte de Lautréamont, he understood. Maldoror's songs, black humor, drastic shifts in tone and style, a kiss of unstoppable evil forsaking God and all of mankind at once in the violent, black storyline. I'm keeping friends close and enemies closer. Plus, for the first time, I'm really in charge.

It all started with a dream. For me, truth was always in the primal power of rock. I wanted truth. Bang a gong, get it on. Heavy breathing and more guitar - take me! Baby baby don't need your jewels in my frown, sixes and sevens and nines. You got to roll me. But in this dream, they were all in Hell. All of them. Jimi Hendrix and Elvis Presley and Janis Joplin and Brian Jones. John Lennon and Buddy Holly and Jim Morrison along with Eddie Cochran and Stevie Ray Vaughan and Chet Baker. Even Miles Davis and Ella Fitzgerald. I peered into the black tombs and noticed Richie Valens was sharing a cell with Duke Ellington. I lost count of the legends, but I'll never forget the strange radiance, almost a smoke, that glowed around Brian Jones. A purple aura licking around him like flames when he walked, covered in tapestries and the smell of Moroccan incense. Like a prince. He glanced upward, blue eyes remembering what once was the sky. The feelings in a dream are the key to their meaning and I felt like there'd been some kind of mistake. This was an error in the fabric of reality that needed to be mended. The founder of the Rolling Stones did not belong in Hades. Blond haired genius, this one had been mistakenly placed in the abyss. As I walked past Elvis' tomb, the King said that the kid was going to try to escape. That he had powers that the other incarcerated did not possess. A secret plan was being devised unbeknownst to the fiendish Lucifer, and with any luck, the Rolling Stone would take his rightful place in the Kingdom of Heaven.

I awoke in a panic that shifted into a kind of calm realization. I realized that I could save something. Whatever happened during that last acid trip with Billy fortified me with personal power, the force of intention to rewrite reality.

We thought the acid wasn't working, so we decided to eat breakfast. I still lived in that shit studio apartment across from Poppycock, the local bar where all the live bands played. He sat in one of the two stained beige swivel stools across from the counter where I stood pouring cereal into bowls. Fruit Loops with vitamin D milk and black coffee. Music. It was night, and the streetlights shone in through the big bay window, the only reason I rented the place apart from access to my favorite bar. The walls had eyes, and the building felt hungry for human contact which is a different infestation from a haunting. Less curable. I was talking to Billy about it; he smoked a cigarette and didn't appear to listen. "The spirit of a lonely place is called wendigo but the Ojibwa, in their folklore, also describe the similar word, windigo as a cannibalistic giant, something one might transform into after consuming human flesh. Most delirium induced states are culture specific syndromes. For instance, the chupacabra, or 'goat sucker', is a doglike beast that drinks the blood of livestock, leaving the corpse intact like a bloodless shell, and is rarely seen by anyone other than Spanish speaking peoples."

"First we drop rip-off acid and now you're talking cryptozoology? Fuck." Billy stared down at the scarred counter top.

"I got it from a couple of kids at the museum. They were dressed in brown fur and long pink and brown doggy ears for a puppy play fetish convention and wanted me to drop the tabs with them right then and there in front of Pollock and everyone, but I had plans. They said I should save it for later." I slid his bowl of cereal full of milk down the island, he caught it. I noticed his pupils were dilated.

He chewed noisily on the cereal and his face changed into an open mouthed grimace like a Kabuki theater mask. "You've fed me broken glass! The fuck, why." The cereal fell out of his mouth onto the table and he mistook his own saliva mixed with food coloring for blood. "I'm bleeding! You bitch! I need to get on the roof."

Billy climbed out the window and up the ladder to the roof, and I had to follow. The acid was working on me too, but having a different effect, sending me down a different street. My bare feet sent fire alarms to the rest of my body as they touched the cold metal of the rungs, the climbing too hyper real, my white knuckled hands gripping the steel looked pale, skeletal and ridiculous, not things I could count on at all.

The asphalt shingles on the roof were still holding the sun's heat, denying the cool dark of the evening that had gone so wrong. I heard a band tuning up at Poppycock. Simultaneously I saw Billy on the edge of the roof. He'd taken off his shoes and socks and, with a look of terror and rage, threw them off the edge of the building like it was the footwear that was wrong, the bleeding mouth trip replaced by a new distrust.

A great rocker hit my ears, the percussion intro filled with anticipation like a knife spreading jam across hot toast, back and forth, back and forth. One touch of my hand on Billy's arm and he was sitting down. Our bare feet dangled over the edge of the house. We looked down at them, swinging our legs to the music. I knew this was a state of fragile grace as I stared down at Poppycock's glowing white marquee with mismatched letters that seemed to shift and fade, reading the band's name was now impossible. It was the space between the notes, really. Sometimes I think Billy and I still live there in that place outside of time where the electric guitar sound is still ringing out between those chords, an arching bridge between

134

notes where two people forever stand. I held my breath through that fractured panic, sensing that this achingly beautiful song could fall apart at any moment.

And when it did, I was ready. The end of the song was abrupt and the night responded by suddenly growing colder. Hands on Billy, leading him slowly down the ladder. For something to be regrettable, something must be lost. We lost a connection to magic, madness, music, sex, love, imagination and replaced it with the small change of managing existence. That was the day I knew.

I knew I could move between these worlds. That pendulum swinging between the ridiculous and the sublime. Organized religion felt like the next best move to me, since I never had my feet firmly planted in either, the world of the magic of existence and the world of control and manipulation. I could do both, and neither location would ever fully have me. Join the church and leave it at the same time.

And what of the Virgin? What is she thinking?

They were in Hell. All of them.

Life Is Solicitation

Masterson would like to film a mass suicide of ten million people. Let's hasten the inevitable, she thought. Leave the corpses for the capitalists to clean up. Bury the people upright like parking meters. Put quarters down their throats. Let the meter maids empty the metal colostomy bags. A suicide will always be known for the final act they committed, their humanity flattened by their exit strategy. Looking down at the sidewalk and, one foot in front of the other, listening to the rhythm of her gate played out with high heel percussion, she thought about that judgment. Everyone commits little suicides against themselves every day to a greater or lesser extent -- every moment of self-doubt, every humiliation, and every moment where subjugation is allowed. Make a large gesture in this direction, take the trip all the way and you're a suicide forever, but it's the same song everyone else sings at a slower tempo. Speed up the song and take that final punk rock leap and you're tragic.

A fly rides a snowflake, a winged maggot on a magic carpet of frozen water. An illumination of consciousness. Masterson ducked into a cafe when the snow came down harder and the sidewalks got slick. Sometimes destruction comes like a mist out of peripheral vision, the space between the words, the forgotten blank awful places people can't be bothered to examine. She opened Akemi's letter after ordering a coffee. "I'm not going to start with that number 23 business. I'm done with it, but it's not done with me." As an art collector, she'd gone to an exhibit while she was in Tokyo five years before.

The gallery was steel and glass. Wrapped packages hung from wires like Christos. She picked Akemi's painting, hidden under the paper, sight unseen. The currency was secrets. All she had to do was write one down, and the artwork was hers. The artwork contained, reciprocally, a secret from Akemi that she wouldn't fully *understand until much later.*

Eye screws, wire and a well-placed guess at where the nail should enter the wall and the painting was hanging in her hallway. Three stylized figures in black, blue and purple. The Toy Manufacturer. Akemi's secret was written on the back. "The middle figure is Johnny, he's the Toy Manufacturer, and the painting is named after him. I met him in a dream."

Back in Tokyo, Akemi was learning about Masterson's secret. No great reveal, just her not-widely-known preoccupation with the number 23 and all its coincidences. He switched on the radio and turned it up. Yes! It was Candy's new single, "Buddha Don't Live in New York City." Akemi was a fan of this new departure in her career, heavily influenced by psych rock and bands like Acid Mother's Temple and the Cosmic Inferno. Thirteen minutes of droning electric guitars punctuated with vocals delivered in a repetitive howl:

Buddha don't live in New York City
Mrs. Claus is a white slut
God is a heart attack
Howl blue
Howl blue
Howl blue

Akemi had a shift in perception similar to déjà vu. Combing through Masterson's message, he thought about the 23 enigma and Psalm 46 (2*23) has as its 46th word "SHAKE" and the 46th word from the end of the Psalm, back to end is "SPEAR". Was Shakespeare 46 when the King James Bible was published? He would have to investigate. William Shakespeare was born on April 23, 1564 and died on April 23, 1616. That's two 23's again...

Howl blue

Howl blue

Howl blue

Back in the states, Masterson was troubled by dreams. She was always in the same house, not hers, but the dream logic told her she lived there. Every night vision took place in the living room. She'd wander in a daze, a sleepwalker in her own dream, picking up brightly colored pieces of plastic off the carpeting in the night of the space. She put them on the mantle, and realized two pieces fit together. She twisted and locked two tubes of plastic, one red and one blue, together to form what looked like a toy dachshund. The next night the dream would continue, more prefab plastic pieces put together to form mismatched brightly colored animals.

Back in Tokyo, Akemi was aware of confirmation bias. He'd see 23 everywhere repeatedly because he was focusing on it, yet he couldn't silence the thoughts. After giving blood, an Internet search revealed that it takes human blood 23 seconds to circulate through the body. After watching a television program about the history of nuclear power, he read that the uranium isotope used in nuclear bombs is U235. He started staying home on the 23rd of each month. When the paralysis began to interfere with his daily routine, he decided to write to Masterson.

Akemi's first letter arrived the morning after a very troubling turn of events in the dark house dreams Masterson had been experiencing each night. This time, she walked down a staircase to the silent evening of the living room once again and spotted through the darkness the objects on the mantle, and then she jumped. Hanging on to the railing, her eyes adjusting to the obscurity of night, she crouched down and noticed a man standing in front of the fireplace examining the plastic toys and putting them in a white bag. He turned to face her. Alarmed, Masterson noticed his large, watery blue eyes which made him look surprised or like a baby bird. His long straight nose drew a line down the middle of his round face. Then he spoke.

"Why did you take the painting down?"

"What?"

"The painting in the hall. The Toy Manufacturer, where is it?"

"I took it to the frame shop, ah..."

"I'm Johnny."

"Johnny the Toy Manufacturer? You don't look like him."

"Yes. Operating among dreams with very low overhead, getting the sleepers to do my work for me. You need to put the painting back where it was."

It was 7pm when Masterson finally decided to call the number Akemi provided in the letter. It was 12:00 pm in Tokyo when Akemi answered the phone.

"I can help you with the 23 Enigma if you can get Johnny off my back."

One hour and forty-five minutes later, Masterson learned that Akemi had similar dreams after executing the Toy Manufacturer painting. In Akemi's dream, he was in a similar living room with a mantle covered in the mismatched disassembled toys. He painted Johnny but the stylized representation didn't suit his dream character's wishes. "In the following dreams I see him, in the dark, out the bay window. He held a sign like at a protest demanding a more representational portrait. In that dream the white ceramic bust of Beethoven flew off the grand piano and smashed against the window." The dream poltergeist caused Akemi to paint Johnny the way he really was in the dream, curly blond hair, bird eyes and round face. He included some of the toys and the white bag in the background just to get it right, along with the ceramic shards of Beethoven's face.

"The dreams stopped then, but I had to get rid of the painting.

I put it in the exhibit in Tokyo and you gave me your secret. I have the more representational portrait hanging in my hall."

Masterson bought that one. No more secrets. Cash. Her dreams stopped, too.

Secrets are dangerous, and art secrets will put you in someone else's story.

I must be losing my mind
Bent sun scarred plastic recycle bins speak English
The wooden deck wanted to converse
The leaves falling from the trees
Were musical sounds
Beethoven would be envious
Miniature movements of varying melody
As if birds had turned to water
But they were not evocative of any composition
They were singular notes
And as any music major should be aware
Singular notes have little value of their own.

Silence is the Alien's First Commandment – Thou Shalt Shut the Fuck Up

"Listen to me, kid. You have the power to control your own thoughts, even if they are delusional. That's real power. The system can throw anything at you in an attempt to annihilate you."

"That's power?"

"The most powerful. All is concept in a capitalistic society where one god rules from absentia. Say you go bankrupt. Big fucking deal. Jettison the concept of guilt."

"It's too easy."

"Too easy? Are you daft? It's the hardest thing in the world to achieve. We'll squeeze out the banks and invent our own type of trade commodity. Our own economy."

"If shit were a commodity, poor people would be born without assholes."

"Ah...ok." Billy relented. "The pig power structure just shifts a little, I get it."

"If I don't believe in my mother, does she disappear?"

"Yes."

There once was a ghost so airy

It got to a virgin named Mary

Christ was so bored

At seeing ma whored

That he set himself up as a fairy.

Did you know? There are some doors in Las Vegas that are never opened. This is new money power. Federal marshals walk by and never knock. Viva Las Vegas. Billy noticed, "One of the Getty heirs had dead chicks hanging from hooks at the MGM Grand."

Dead bodies are easy. The Getty Villa wasn't a big enough museum for the Standard Oil fucks. They needed it bigger and *better. Travertine, from the quarry called Bagni di Tivoli in Italy was imported to southern California in a quantity equivalent to 108,000 square meters to build the bigger, better monument. Climb up to the Getty Center and dig the twigs and leaves from ancient times impressed into this limestone, deposited by mineral springs, particularly hot springs. The vegetation is long gone but waves hello, imprinted in stone while the public walks up those narrow stairs to view the art. Narrow stairs the right size for the old white people to hoist their girth up to the Expressionist room to see Edvard Munch's "Starry Night" and James Ensor's "Christ's Entry Into Brussels in 1889." Do the visitors ever see themselves in Ensor's perverse masked faces ignoring the haloed Christ, humble and demure in the center of the canvas parade? What do we have here, chaos, indulgence, self-obsession and even a bare ass shitting off the edge of a balcony? Christ who?*

Remember the Mama Cass doll with the ham sandwich accessory? The Kennedy doll with the exploding skullcap. The Lennon Five Shot see-through figurine. New York City squad car and Yoko Ono sold separately.

The Blood Queen Time Travel Spaceways Incorporated was franchised through Candy, God's daughter, for time travel purposes. Once the public could move between years, there were no more conversations about regret, regret about missing the Clash opening for the Who in 1982, the Flying Burrito Brothers live in 1969 or the

Beatles at Shea Stadium on August 2, 1966. Concert time travel was big business. A byproduct of time travel/practical time/space saver became the psychic air jet that functioned based on its occupants belief in its ability to operate as an airplane. More time saved-no luggage, no fuel to support the aircraft which possessed no gravity. Train yourself to hold your hand out palm upward in front of you at eye level, imagine your toothbrush, it appears in your hand. Toss it up in the air again, and it disappears. So it goes with your hairbrush, your shaving kit, your makeup bag, your clothing. The palm of the hand at eye level while thinking of the object needed, its appearance, and a toss in the air to make it vanish into invisible storage. Same with the plane. Everyone boards, sits, waits. Masterson's first psychic air jet trip was at night. She looked down at the stars, her legs swinging beneath her skirt in the cool air, barefoot with no concerns. She believed in all her luggage so it would be there for her when she shot out her palm to conjure her toiletries, brush her teeth and go to bed in a new town thousands of miles from where she elevated at 30,000 feet with others who believed in the same outcome.

Plane crashes were eliminated during the boarding process through the use of shamans who boarded passengers based on their lifespan. The person waiting to board with the shortest lifespan, in other words the next person to die, would be able to board first. Next came the second person to die, and so on. The last person to board had the longest experience on earth compared to the rest, and thus had time to spare. The dates of death and the span of passenger life were never revealed explicitly, it was merely an efficient queuing theory developed by statisticians and holy men. However, on rare occasions, the shamans noted that the death day/lifespan of all the passengers was equal and imminent. In other words, they'd all cracked some kind of code in the shaman's magic to die at the same time. In case of this rare anomaly, the flight was cancelled. The crash seemed almost certain and completely avoidable.

Picasso was such a rotten bastard, short too. He lived to be twice as old as your Christ. Warhol was a manipulative American/Czechoslovakian homosexual, rewarded for the reprise. "Let's go, I've seen enough of man and his art."

"In a bear market the devil buys souls."
"Have you lost your fucking mind?"
"Pull your skirt up, I'm going to spank you."
"I'm the Blood Queen, asshole."
"Do as you're told or you'll be fucked, also!"
"Guards!"
Slowly, the pain began to accompany her to the Theatre. It was too late for doctors. Too late for booze and drugs and love. To late even for Satan and his flying all-star fiasco, sitting in the back row at a Kenneth Anger Theremin concert performance in downtown Los Angeles among the perfumed crowd under red light, the

Complete Magick Lantern Cycle projected over the stage. She kissed all the boys goodbye. Six overweight virgins carried her onto the airplane. The corpse flew first class and was later hacked to pieces in Cuba, like the cedar and tropical mahogany trees felled by the Spanish conquistadors there long ago, the forest island rendered flat. Resources exploited and used up too quickly. You will know there is no God when the cold yellow sun refuses to shine.

The Mean Tubes

"Jesus Christ, Billy; You take this shit too seriously."

"Perhaps you're right."

"That's right, you know, there is no truth, everything is permitted."

"You're a sadistic young bastard, Morrison."

"Help me, Billy," said Morrison Clown.

A doctor claims that shame is a physiological response. I passed on his book to many others.

"Which one is Kerouac's grave?"

"It's the one with all the garbage in front of it."

Morrison Clown learned to deconstruct popular music from his mentor. But, when it evolved to discussing the actual notes, whether this note or that was a rock and roll note, Billy remained silent because he didn't know how to read or make musical notation. A lesson well learned from Ludwig, mad composer Beethoven pissing in a chamber pot under his piano, composing long after he failed to hear the notes. Then he decided to deconstruct The Holy Bible in search of the flaw, the flaw that had to be discovered to free him.

"Show me your asshole, or I'll take you into that church." And the boy's mother pointed toward the cathedral, and reached into her purse and pulled out a glazed buttermilk donut.

"If I show you my anus, how can I be sure?"

"How can you be sure I won't eat this donut?"

"Look, mother, I would tell you if some queer priest was trying to stick my shit."

"Drop those pants now."

"I'm starting to worry about you mom."

"Hey, your father and I were instrumental in getting this policy passed with the cooperation of the school and the diocese."

"You're a bunch of sick fucks."

"It's the only way to be absolutely sure that your asshole has not been violated."

"OK mom, you win. But I should warn you that we had corn and wine last night at Bible School."

And then the woman made the sign of the cross and started to scream "The one eyed stink hole of Satan, show mother the brown stink eye of Lucifer. Save me from the satanic sex hole. Repeat after me, 'Save me from the satanic sex hole.'"

"Save me from the satanic sex hole."

"Louder."

"Save me from the satanic sex hole." And then she pried open his anus with a plastic disposable crucifix. She splashed the orifice with a cotton swab dipped in holy water and checked for flesh contamination and spermatozoa. The results were instantaneous. Father appeared at the front door with the gift wrapped suppositories.

"And how does the boy look, Gladys?"

"He's negative, Vernon, negative as the Lord is Great."

Bible School's corn and wine was the least of it. Every summer they'd send their smiling yellow buses through the slums and pick up kids in rags with dirty faces. In bible school, singing songs, having cookies and punch and that entire attention--wait. What? Uncle Bob said we should tithe. It wasn't just a shakedown, it was a competition. The kids were divided into teams. Parted like the Red Sea. Each team had a golden chalice near the pulpit. Whoever had the most in tithes per day would "win". Uncle Bob, the missionary in charge of that bible school that summer, encouraged everyone to look for loose change under the cushions of the couches of their parent's home. Look in the car between the seats. Look everywhere. You want your team to win, yes? The money goes to missions. Whoever brings the most coin wins.

That's when the poor kids really looked defeated. Defeated and under pressure. Out of place, those feelings were familiar.

Halfway through the week a 7 year old girl went home from bible school and told her parents over dinner that she was worried. Worried that the chalice/coin collection competition was making some of the kids feel bad because they didn't have the spare change to give to God and his missionaries.

Her father leaned in and said, with a grimace resembling a scowl, "The money doesn't go to God, it doesn't go to missions, it goes to Uncle Bob."

"What? So he takes that loose change and buys whatever he wants?"

"YES."

Armed with this new information, the girl spread the news, whispered behind her hand into an ear, the ripple effect felt immediately. The teams, quickly, stopped shaking down their families for loose change. Uncle Bob took down the golden chalices and eventually stopped talking about it. The game shut down.

One law officer is killed in the line of duty in this country every thirty-nine hours. "Which begs the question?"

"Don't," said Morrison Clown.

"Why does it take almost two days?" There were two Township officers sitting in the greasy restaurant. "Because they are uneducated and under trained," said Billy, as he began to rise from the yellow and chrome stool, loose change once in the hands of Uncle Bob dancing and bouncing across the coffee stained grey Formica counter top.

"Easy Billy," said Morrison with a most uneasy white smile.

"Can you smell that?"

"Billy, not now please...I'm trippin'."

Billy turns toward the officers and eye contact is made. "Can you smell that? Smells like death to me." This hatred of authority is both genetic and learned behavior, due to external mental programming. A combination of white slave genetics and motion pictures.

Art dealers are like Satan; A necessary evil to keep the illusion and myth alive. And High School Sally flashed through his mind as someone who should be used and then abused, and all her money thrown to corporate piranhas in the holy name of religion and law. (That's not really true, he was thinking about reciprocity and nuclear bridges and sacred virgin thighs, and birth marks, and a drunken night of pawing a bloody fat coeducational sex machine in the land of hamburgers and airplanes and green lawns.)

"Release her name." He said nothing, he continued to type. "Release her name now? I demand it!"

"Sally Synthesis."

"I will not put up with your insubordination." She reached for the phone and moments later said, "This is a code red, send Veronica and the nurses down to section O-23," and she threw the cell phone against the wall. "Perhaps a half hour with the sadistic Dr. Rose and Associates will free your tongue," she said with a combination of hatred and glee. Her white teeth were smeared with lipstick and chocolate. Her small knuckles were as white and hard as slave diamonds. "It's out of my hands, mind punk."

When the torture session was over, after the electrodes were snapped to his nuts with rusted alligator clips and the electric cattle prod rammed into his shaved anus, and after the smoke and stench cleared, he was wrapped in honey, fire ants and force fed seven rotted, maggot infested pork chops...Only then did she return to the examining room and asked one simple question. "Perhaps I can have the name now?" But there was no answer.

The Mean Tubes gathered around the black stretch limousine to count their money. The women were all gone. The Satellites called it Gynecological Genocide. Murdered, and later sodomized on replica post fences from the *Bonanza* television set. The corpses were eventually ground into unusable stem cells and still later converted to fertilizer. In the year 2526, the Mean Tubes turned on the Digital Detectives, and when the President was found huddled in a closet masturbating to a Xerox copy of the original Articles of Confederation, that's when the computers knew the gig was up and began a systemic destruction of all Robotic Life Forms (RLF). The toasters as well as Mabel the inflatable fuck maid — all were eliminated equally with extreme prejudice.

In the bloody and smoldering bio-electro-chemical aftermath, all that remained were the Mean Tubes and the Computer Christ. A total of thirteen Digital Detectives managed to remain alive and active in the virus underground. To be found with a woman or a female robot or any feminine gargoyle or flesh clone or artificial fuck hole was a violation of satellite law and offenders were subjected to immediate public execution, always well attended.

"Who owns America?" asked Morrison Clown.

"You can't take the weight of the world on your shoulders. You'll go mad like Montgomery Clift. You don't want to go crazy like Montgomery Clift, do you?"

"Who owns America?"

"Hold that thought. The great flaw in Christianity is that the body is gone. When you die your body stays here, and some soul or ghost or some fucking nonsense floats to another world or plane. Where is the body, Christian? Find the body and shatter the whole concept of gods once and for all. Forget life after death, is there life before death?"

The Computer Christ owns America. You have to believe his hard drive crashed and his motherboard transferred and reborn into another machine.

I was talking
When I should have been listening
I didn't hear a word that anyone said

Hüsker Dü, the Zen Arcade Album, 1984. Too much punk rock was "Fuck you," but here we have a rare case of "Fuck me." What's going on inside my head?

"But why evoke Montgomery Clift?"
Morrison Clown and Billy in the year 2526. The Christ motherboard transfer secured down the superhighway with no exits or speed limits.
"Because the Mean Tubes are all descendants of the great homosexual actor. They were all cloned from his DNA. He was considered one of the most beautiful specimens of the male species."

He's an airplane, baby
Don't forget it
He's an airplane, baby
He's jet fuel from the new school
Don't forget it
He's jet fuel from the new school
He's an airplane, baby
Don't forget it

He's an airplane, baby

He's an airplane

Cloning for the Spiritual and Religious by Habib Radackovich, D.D.S. Part time scientist and occasional religious zealot, the dentist from Detroit via Montenegro takes us on a journey to the heart of genetics and God. Leave your blue screen, this is the real illusion. Dr. Radackovich weaves a fascinating tale of the discovery of Jesus Christ's skeleton and the attempted cloning of The Savior. The kidnapping of the baby clone, and its virtual crucifixion, will leave the reader mortified and in a state of permanent psycho-stigmata. This New Handbook of Freedom is beginning to see the light, or to shoot them out one by one and institute darkness forever, not sure which. "Do almost anything at any time."

"That's wild, man."

"Or else I'll be melancholic, too."

"I don't want this virus in my house."

When gold backing was withdrawn in the early twentieth century, that's when the words In God We Trust started to be printed on the money. On the money. Another faith-based proposition. They all got together and decided they could no longer trust in gold, so they turned to another illusion, a new golden calf to worship. I'm set free to find a new illusion...

"That's Lou Reed," Morrison Clown said.

154

We've all got to find a new place to lock ourselves up the minute we get free. That mind virus is a hard one to break. The phone rang. He picked it up after the first ring. A black woman asked for him and in the process butchered his name. He immediately hung up, but the virus was planted and took many forms, including this writing. But reader, you're so silent. The first thing to say in response is to demand that they introduce themselves. This throws the telephonic scum off guard.

I'll tell you who my current long distance provider is, as long as you call me 'Captain' at the beginning of every sentence, or whenever you address me directly. Do something for me, and I'll do something for you. Or, tell them you'll listen to their spiel if they sing their question to the tune of The Battle Hymn of the Republic. Make the fuckers hang up on YOU. We are all trapped in an economic theory. Presentation is key. Glory, glory, hallelujah! "Goodbye."

"No, I'm serious, Billy. You know you hate this country."

"I'm the last patriot, asshole. Never forget it."

"You have some strange ways of showing it."

"Patriots are born from dissonance."

Go to Mark Twain National Forest. Check out the trees. Think about the fact that American traditionalists are an outdated, forgotten, obsolete format. Mark Twain touted the notion that the government should act as an engine driving the needs of the people. The Digital Christ tries to make you forget what you need most to remember, remember and wonder when the concept of true representation became antiquated.

Gave my name to the wrong guy
He does not look like the FBI
Gave my number to the wrong guy
A white republican named Sly.

Gave my number to the wrong chick
Hope she does not have a dick
Gave my number to the blind prick
Found him murdered, beaten with a stick.

Cry until next Thursday
Cry until Good Friday
Cry the night away
Cry, cry the night away

Gave my cash to my baby
The brunette, the white lady
Gave my cash to the church crazy
The blond, the Korean's shady.

Gave my God away to Walmart

Not the bankrupt Kmart

Gave my God away at the false start

Like the bulimic with the Pop Tart.

Cry until the bombs drop

Cry for the inflatable cop

Cry the night away

Cry, cry the night away

Replace another motherboard.

More Advice on Dealing With Phone Solicitors

Thirty five million years of evolution and that in of itself is reason to believe that man was the wrong choice. What value is inherent in studying the last two thousand years or the last two thousand days? Morrison said "When I was a child I didn't understand why they would invent words like misanthropic or misogynistic. I couldn't comprehend hatred." Billy smiled and walked toward a yellow cab. It began to rain and the kid purchased a red umbrella on the smelly silver grey streets of Memphis, Tennessee. Time to take the ride. Be prepared.

Masterson abuses the kid and Billy is nonplussed, but Morrison is suffering from a case of massive guilt, an accelerated obsession that threatens to dismantle the heist.

There is a knock on the motel door. Billy is downtown, and the kid is watching college football on an old black and white television while getting stoned. High football thoughts: Why all the matching clothes and no singing and dancing? They can all afford their own football, why fight over one?

"Yeah, yeah hold on there motherfucker," mumbles Morrison.

Opening the door, he says "No, ah. Who are?"

"Sorry, Nancy Masterson," and she rudely stares at his crotch, then laughs. "Open this bastard," she demands, and hands the kid a bottle of beer.

"Sure lady, hell. Have a seat, too."

She takes a huge gulp of the beer and sits on the ugly green bedspread. "When do you expect Billy?" She readjusts herself and pulls her dress past her thighs, nearly exposing her crotch. She crosses her legs.

"Not for an hour at least, make yourself comfortable. Care for some smoke?"

"Sure," and as she lights a number they smoke and drink and watch football.

"Show me."

"Huh?"

Masterson laughs, "Stand up and show me your cock."

"Stand up and show me your pussy," he says while squinting, choking in an attempt to talk while holding the smoke in his lungs. They both laugh.

"I won't ask you nicely again."

"Fuck off, lady."

Masterson stands and pulls the kid into her arms. She fumbles with his jeans and says "Show me the god in your pants," then rips them down to his knees. The kid's lips turn into a smile, and she latches on to the elastic waistband of his white briefs and they quickly follow. Morrison, not to be outdone, lifts her summer dress over her head and she is topless except for white cotton panties. She suddenly grabs his cock and says "It's been a long time since I had a boy's ass across my lap." Morrison starts to protest, but Masterson has tightened her grip around his cock and he is a helpless child. She whispers in his ear, "I said it's been a long time since I spanked the daylights out of a young boy's ass."

"Ah, miss. Ah..."

"Assume the position."

"Ah, lady can't we ah talk."

"Now!" she demands, tightening her squeeze as his knees buckle and he's lying across her thighs. "Understand something, kid. I'm going to warm your ass red, and then you're going to suck me off, do you understand?"

Morrison thought of his options, and as she continued to tighten her grip, he replied "Yes, yes whatever you say." Then she raised her lovely arm in the air and spanked his stoned cheeks a brilliant red, all the while holding on to his now erect cock. When she finished she commanded him onto his knees to service her pussy. Morrison was definitely beaten. He worked his tongue and lips eagerly on her sour summer box and was reduced to a sex slave in moments. She came in minutes, dressed and left with the kid holding his cock in his hand, his ass the color of a cherry red GTO.

The next time you are annoyed with a telemarketing scum mother, read the above paragraph aloud to them, tell them you're masturbating to their offer while recording their reaction, and then play it back to them. **Somebody is listening to you.**

The National Institute of American Psychiatry has labeled your spanking novella as pornographic, and its author as an obsessive and schizophrenic reprise of bipolarity.

"That's one of the better reviews," *and he laughed at his own joke.* "You remind me of the King of Rock and Roll, Chuck Berry. He was sometimes lost in the public self-conscious. Exposed too much."

"Mr. Ball, you have a minor best seller at best, have you affected the day?"

He swears to the courtroom that he has Van Gogh's ear lobe in a tiny jar filled with colored formaldehyde.

Keep a grip on your serotonin and dopamine levels. "Exactly. How the hell do you do that without a prescription from your local general practitioner? For the poison Benzoid of your choice?"

"Are you aware that Ritalin opens the same brain receptors as cocaine? What you have now are children wired from pre-school with a brain so damaged and the rewiring so haphazard that it's just a matter of time before this witches brew boils over and scalds all in positions of authority."

All the kids are eating every chemical. This is the result of undetected molecular changes occurring in the genome. Hatching hearts in the heart factory. Growing a mind in the old glory straight jacket of power propaganda.

"I want everyone to *be* like America, and never admit any culpability." (laughter)

Except they didn't laugh. They sat in rows, motionless. The interrogation continued. "Is your novella hidden with secret messages of hate?"

"No."

"I'll ask you one more time, is your novella a diatribe of hate and misogyny and misanthropic vomit hurled at the American people and their right to practice the religion of their choice?"

"No, definitely not."

"Isn't all of your writing one continuous slur of disgust hurled at all authority and every decent human on this planet?"

"Please don't confuse my persona with any of your socio-religious metaphors."

Billy seemed frozen to his chair while a doctor in a white coat approached him from the left, rolled up Billy's sleeve and produced a syringe. He searched for a vein while the interrogator stated "No one has time for this anymore. It'll be just like taking a nap, Mr. Ball. Endless sleep. Guilty on all charges."

He sat upright in the backseat with a start and, covered in sweat, asked Morrison "How long have I been out?" Morrison read the yellow cab meter. "You've been out $42.75 worth, Billy."

Perception is a copy

Consciousness a mimeograph

Algebraic abstraction

Wonderland

Alice

The Key to Pop Riches

Some scientists say the color of the universe is turquoise or some hue in the green blue wavelength. Perhaps an experiment with infinite color illusions in conjunction with the new figure/ground.

"Saint Augustine turned sex into sin around 400 years after the death of the miracle man," said Billy Ball.

"Here we go," said the Kid. "I'm a Christian, and some of this offends my Baptist sensibilities."

"Grow up, cunt. I'm not trying to poison you."

"Poison me? Baptists are God's favorite. You're the cunt. I fell asleep during the fire and brimstone sermons and had dreams of hell. I bet you've never seen the place."

"Don't make this personal. Saint Augustine destroyed sexuality. And all you blind, holy body crossing brainwashed American religious zealots follow a hoot of words that were bastardized from the start. God hides on the molecular level. He's much worse than Mike Tyson. He'll swallow the ear, and after his morning toilet, show it to the victim, if possible. You're lost, kid. Lost in a sea of mirrors and televisions."

The insects were capable of morphing themselves into common debris. They became what they ingested. The insects were resilient to all chemical poisons. Consciousness is a postulate. Learn to live with snakes.

"Man will fuck up eternity," said Billy.

"That's rude."

"Yes, it is."

How high can you fly? Will the virus survive? Answer me you sedated motherfucker! Don't make me invoke the evil white one. Kiss my feet you Christian fool, you holy goof, you ego fuck.

"Can one escape metaphysical planes?"

"Only one way, kid."

Morrison Clown was ill, but we already knew that. He turned on the radio and lost his mind. Candy knows, sings it, too! The key to pop riches is to mock your father. It's now or never.

Blame it on Castro, that asshole

Blame it on the Beatles, that freak show

Blame it on Oswald, that sad clown

Blame it on McVeigh, by the way

Blame it on...you get the picture

That is to say that semantics conveys image and not presence

(Candy's Blame Rap, you know you bought the digital download.)

What is Language?

What is God?

What is Hope?

What is a Heart?

Nothing.

Come on.

Do you hear those joy bells?

Jesus was a gun runner.

Say it isn't so.

Lost Rembrandt, where are you?

We'll use this instead.

You redundant fuck (repeat fifteen times while Candy burns a reproduction of Albrecht Dürer's Praying Hands pen and ink drawing onstage between the dancers who orbit the flames.)

Please stop

Van Gogh fucked your God in the ass

Stop it, please

No anus was safe from the golden pig

Her pleas fell on no ear

And have I told you lately that I love you

Darling, I beg of you

Remove your clothes

Is your love forever

Fuck no

I can't go on

Remove your clothes

I won't ask you again

It makes no difference

I hear a saxophone in the distance. The sound splashes. You're sure to lose the blues in Memphis. "Let's follow the horn," I said. "Half block away." I start to walk, fast. He follows with a smile on his face. Tiny crystals first melt and then cry on his collar. Cold rain. He speaks.

"Do you fucking believe this shit? It's a blind dog convention."

"Your God, blind indeed."

The kid went mad in the mansion. Trying on Elvis' clothes, the gold lame, the army uniform, the black comeback leathers. He didn't touch the piano. Turned on all three television sets with the volume muted. He imagined himself in the sergeant's uniform. "Presley" says the cloth name tag.

Hard wired technology represents the last bastion of privacy, and they are all going digital. In the year of the digital, privacy evaporates. This is terminal evaporation. Gone Elvis. The tin foil and black out drapes are still intact. Should we give him a proper name? LOVE THY NEIGHBOR. What? Was your God tripping that day? Digging bar. Two guys, dirt, concrete, sledgehammer to the concrete lid. Presto. Unlock the casket, two locks on the front of the lid. There's Elvis.

There's hate that lived in that place, a palpable hate. The failure of the commandments is a blasphemy coded together through six million television screens blinking Morse code messages we have no receptors to receive. There is a text that says Elvis Presley never had intercourse with Priscilla after Lisa Marie was born. Strange. Billy told the kid that it was because he didn't want to be known as a motherfucker. Death came too soon and was black, ugly, and room temperature.

Since Graceland, he could not shake loose the feelings of death that floated around his being. His aura was infected. He sensed the end coming. Bring down the curtain; there will not be an encore. Although there existed an outside chance of the metaphysical reality espoused by millions of believers that in fact life after death was possible and wholly probable. The kid believed it, Billy did not. He thought mankind too inherently corrupt and dirty. That all the myths were in reality false truths and that man could not be free until this terrible mind virus was erased and annihilated from the planet.

Since Graceland, Billy knew he was marked. Something

would happen. The heist went south partly because of all the frozen moments spent in the planning stages. Too much talk and not enough action hasten failure. The words cling to you, that's part of the mind virus deal. Words are small mouth noises sending code to other receptors. All these sound shapes caved in on us, we carried all these expectations along for the ride when we should have jettisoned them, learned them and forgotten them and act with perfect clarity. The way of the Samurai. Who was he kidding; they never had clarity, just the mud of words that couldn't amount to decisive action. The blur of memory colliding with the present.

Masterson was locked in that same madness linked to the perils of memory. She'd finished her postulancy, tested for six months and made the cut in the convent. It felt easy. The vows of poverty, who cares? Modern life on the outside was a never ending cycle of poverty. The chastity, the obedience, that was the tricky stuff. The daily recitations of the liturgy took her mind off it for the most part, but the walls separating her from the outside world couldn't stop the flood. Personal histories in the flood. One event happened, and another, and the more time passed, it blurred and overlapped with the present and what should be the new. The repetition of memory, of revisiting moments in the past again and again -- she knew she was just remembering the last time she thought about Billy, the last time she sat at a bar and listened to Candy's hit song while drinking beer, the last time she remembered fucking college boys, vacuuming her apartment, hailing a cab. She could never get back to the memory exactly; it's just in the soup. Unrecoverable. Masterson felt her mind splitting.

Enjoy the obsession

Of fictional biography

Sing the words sinner

Glory to war and destruction

Come

Praise the gun

Applaud the bomb

Let us adore

The end of man

Amen

FOURTEEN

After making love I did the unthinkable.   I asked Parker to marry me.

"What?"

"Marry me...tonight...now...right fucking now."

"Billy...please...stop fooling around."

I grabbed the yellow Glad Twist Tie that held my hair in place...and she blushed strawberry...and she hesitantly offered her left hand.

"No...Not the left...we're going Eastern Orthodox...give me your right hand...because God made nothing with his left."   I twisted the plastic around her right ring finger and said, "Marry me Parker...please..."

I did not go on bended knee...to hell with that...she looked at the faux ring...and said, "Yes Billy, I'll be your Bride."

"Now...let's do this...hurry...there's a Bridal Shop at the San Remo hotel...here's ten thousand...buy something exquisite...use the cross walks...I'll be in the sports bar wearing an Yves Saint Laurent tux."

Parker kissed me passionately and skipped out the door like a schoolgirl.

I rented a tuxedo on the second floor of the MGM Grand...escalated down to the sports book...I did not wager...just watched the late game...Seattle vs. Oakland.   I ordered a super cold Heineken...smiled and waited for my future Bride. Oakland had just kicked a field goal making the game a tie with 11:55 left in the fourth quarter...23 to 23.

Ordering another beer at the bar. Several women were crying and screaming.

"Oh my God...Oh my God...A woman was just run down on Tropicana Avenue...Oh my God...Dear Jesus...she was wearing a Wedding Dress!"

The beer bottle fell silently from my hand onto the bar...foam spraying the bartender...and I ran toward the front door of the Hotel knocking patrons out of the way. In the middle of Tropicana Avenue lay Parker crushed and broken in a three-quarter-sleeve lace cathedral train wedding dress. She was destroyed...she was already dead...there was an ambulance on the scene...and I screamed at the driver to bring me some ice and the emergency kit.

Masterson had the Brian Jones dream again. In the dream he's stuck-- not a multi-instrumentalist, not a blues guitarist, not the founder of the Rolling Stones. No, he's the drowned mad Ophelia, his humanity diminished by one final act, one final accident or one final murder but this was his short byline, nevertheless. Nancy Masterson - Nun. It's other people who decide who we are and she felt summed up. Categorized. She remembered the professor in college who taught performance art as a subset of the aesthetics requirement for her art degree. The assignments were wild and free and anything goes, but some kids didn't have the knack to make a statement. They couldn't hold an audience, couldn't turn it into a standup routine or a music recital or any other form of entertainment. They were young and got too serious. Five o' clock on Friday, and all the assignments needed to be turned in. Some were videotaped, others on after-the-fact art objects describing the event they'd isolated as THE PERFORMANCE. A myriad of creative approaches would be reviewed by the instructor at a later date. He didn't automatically open the envelope that said, on the outside in bold marker block print, READ IMMEDIATELY.

In retrospect, that's the part Masterson never understood. This was an assignment, not an excuse to hijack someone's life. Fortunately, when the professor packed it all in and drove to his vacation home on the lake that evening, he put that particularly urgent envelope on the top of the box. A late night in front of the fire with a glass of wine turned into a nightmare when he read the note and realized that this kid, this fuck up, had buried himself up to his neck in the ground some 50 miles away from where he was sitting and was STILL THERE waiting for his teacher to unearth him with a shovel, at which time he'd planned on reading a poem about trust, and about life after death.

Nine full hours in the cold ground in frigid and ever-decreasing temperatures and the kid was rescued. Masterson never discovered what grade he received for this performance art project prank, but the professor's career was ruined. The faculty voted against keeping him as an adjunct because his ideas and methodologies were now considered dangerous. And there you have it, he never asked for this but welcome to the new world of Who You Are Now.

Brian's heavy lidded blue eyes still looked up seeking the sky. Masterson awoke in sheer terror. She got out her notebook:

I have seen too much.

I have read too much.

Dear God in heaven,

Have the seeds that have been sowed

In this magnificent book,

The Holy Bible,

Are they nothing but mere distortions?

Apparitions.

Anyone who picks up quill or pen making marks with ink

Has an agenda.

Tell me it isn't so.

Why have the Romans all been exonerated in the Gospels?

Is it possible that the Jews did not kill the King?

And that Rome?

Please forgive me, Father.

That Rome and the Vatican

Are Babylon?

History belongs to the conquerors.

Some conceptual artist recorded the White Album in 100 digital overlays.   100 plays of various copies of that vinyl captured, overlapping and compressed on vinyl in 800 copies.   The layering of 100 graffiti scarred *White Album* covers made up the album art. Masterson felt like what this record actually was, she felt like contraband, an unofficial bootlegged version of herself. The writing, stamps, stains and doodles overlap the telltale *White Album* indicator, THE BEATLES, looking out crookedly from decades of 100 albums being used, drawn on, listened to…How many joints were rolled, how many coffee stains and blood stains and dirty fingerprints and food and sick and seed and vomit and shit and "please return to's" and cocaine lines and mud and soot and smears can talk to you at once, all devoted to a finite song selection recorded in the late sixties by twentysomething boys fractured by fame, the Maharishi, and a sense that they were shedding their fab exoskeletons and emerging as something else? Masterson felt these scars of history, the humid compression of multiple recollections as she lived in the convent, listening over and over again to the familiar tunes that over time elapsed on an album side, the phase separation blurred into a soundscape nothing quite like the original songs but somehow familiar yet incomprehensible.

It would be easy. Week five and it's still on constant rotation, the record spinning matching her thoughts that were wound in tight concentric circles.   The larger suitcase would fit the set of encyclopedias that distracted her for the last year and a half, the dictionary, notebooks, and drawings.   The smaller one would

173

contain her meager clothing and toiletries. The static swamp
of Beatle voices and instruments echoing echoing echoing but she'd
leave it there like a manifesto.

She walked out the door with her two suitcases. Masterson was
buried up to her neck no more. Now it's time to say goodnight.

Black

Black

Black

That's all she ever wears.

Or it's

White

White

White.

Never any color

Only colors devoid of hue.

Dear God In Heaven!

Give me some crimson

Or sapphire

Or perhaps a habit of indigo

A robe of aquamarine

Shoes of emeralds and salmon

A collar of apricot

A costume of watermelon

A dress of blood and skim milk

Give me a garment of sunset

Cloth of turquoise and violet

Stockings of lemon

A frock of gold and jealousy

Wrap me in a skirt of traffic lights

Garb of garish orange neon

A uniform of blue eggs

A wardrobe of star matter

The trappings of honey

A sundress of Easter

And a smock of blond hair

Shifts the color of school buses

Threads of auburn silk

Rags of platinum and suburban lawns

Drapes of the Queen of Hearts

Around a gown of verdant virgin

A house dress of lapis lazuli

Perhaps a habit of Selsun Blue

Enough of black and white

Black and white

Enough

I can take no more

Black

and White

"She's gone mister...gone."

"PLEASE...NOW!"

"That's sick, mister."

"SHUT YOUR FUCKIN' MOUTH! JESUS CHRIST! THE GRAND ILLUSIONIST COULD NOT EVEN SAVE HIMSELF."

There's something about seeing a dead body in the road. The animation of life force disappears. What was once a person turns into something inanimate. A bag of potatoes. Stained rags. Broken glass. If you get there before the designated authorities cordon off the area and cover the corpse with a white sheet, you'll see the full show in all its morbid fascination, and you'll slow down to participate, everyone craning their necks, rolling down their windows and saying "How horrible." A traffic jam like a funeral procession, served up instantly like fast food, and just as cheap. Too many times when she was a girl, Parker would be in the back seat of the family station wagon, and the family needed to create a distraction. Her siblings would immerse her attention with a game, or point to a building. "Do you know who lives there?" Usually there was a dead squirrel or rabbit in the road, sometimes even a dog or a cat, and this would cause them to invent a deliberate diversion. They knew if little Parker saw, she'd cry and ask a lot of questions. Did they feel pain? Are they really dead? Dead flowers in a vase had the same effect. Some error must have told her that she'd end up as roadkill. A tear in the membrane of linear time must have let her see things simultaneously, that future, the lace interfacing with rivulets of blood and dirt, forming pools on concrete and silk. This early panic was the only panic she'd have. No procrastinating, she'd got it out of the way early. Dead instantly.

Billy swore he heard a little girl crying in the street.

I held Parker close to me. "I love you Parker," I whispered. I could no longer look. I could no longer stay. I walked away down the center of Tropicana Avenue carrying the bloody emergency kit, cars honking, traffic blocked, people still screaming, and I remembered something she'd said to me the night before.

"It's not the years Billy...It's not the miles...It's the miles per hour."

My faith was gone. I was ready, ready to burn the Cloth of Jesus. I am walking out of this church forever. I gave my bible to Sister Rose. I gave my rosary to Father Thomas.

I called a cab and told the driver to take me away. Climbing in, the smell of leather and cigarette smoke and the residual odors of people and handbags and luggage and transitory movements -- this cab acted like a decompression chamber where I'd wait, an in between place taking me back to the secular world. The cab driver regarded me in his rear view mirror. He was a black man with eyes that registered a concern for my well-being. Hauling human cargo had taught him to read faces and body language and he could see my awkward transformation reflected through the glass. I said stop.

He dropped me off in a lovely park. When I offered to pay the fare, he said no, no money from you, Sister. Still kind eyes of concern that hesitated after I'd shut the door, only eventually driving away. As I walked across the green sculpted lawn, I came upon a beautiful child. She had hair of brown and eyes of black, so black that they radiated a white light. Looking in these eyes, reflective liquid pools, I could see she was somewhat frightened of me. Dressed like a witch in ink, her fear made sense. I smiled at her and asked her name. She smiled back showing a set of teeth like tiny white pearls and said "Maria Olivia." I was so relieved to meet a little girl who seemed so happy, pure and loved. "Where are your parents?" She pointed to a park bench several yards away. I waved to them with the hand of peace and they acknowledged, knowing their child was safe in my presence. I asked the girl to do something for me. She giggled, and with a wave of my hand above her tiny head I told her to dance in a circle, first to the right and then to the left. Maria Olivia started to spin in one direction and then the other, all the while following the commands of my right hand. She had jazz movements hardwired into her DNA, a memory from some past existence in a dark smoky bar listening to Ella Fitzgerald, throwing her head back and laughing with the same abandon she showed now on this day and in this park. Dizzy, she finally fell unceremoniously on her white panty bottom and broke out in laughter. I carefully crouched down, hands on my knees and stared again into her lovely raven eyes, still glistening like black fire. That's when she asked me if I was God. I did not answer her. She asked again, and I whispered through the tears I could no longer hold back, "I represent God. I represent God." The girl looked in my eyes while her child fingers slowly moved my windswept hair away from my face. She tucked the unruly strands behind my left ear and held her tiny hand there for a moment, then turned and skipped away.

ABOUT THE AUTHORS

Nick Vukmanovich is the inventor of Psycho/Social Portraiture for Writing and Painting. An aesthetic facture employing Quad-Conscious (Conscious Subconscious Unconscious and Altered Conscious) methodologies. A psychological and sociological stratagem that demarcates the very definition of art (That which affects the day). In consequence an automobile accident one takes to eternity or a senseless brutal murder is considered art.

Sharon Anderson is a surrealist painter, collagist, arts writer, world traveler, concert attendee and wearer of shiny clothes.

americancockroachnovel@gmail.com